Beth st... ...s
**of Raphael's voice that he was standing
just behind her.**

"Beth?"

She turned to face him, wavering slightly as she found that Raphael was standing only inches away from her, those piercing blue eyes still narrowed in his harshly chiseled face.

Her eyes flashed darkly. "What more do any of you want from me?"

What did Raphael want from this woman?

It was all too easy to imagine making love to her; kissing those delectable and stubborn pouting lips, enjoying and pleasuring those lean, silkily slender curves, caressing and tasting the fullness of her breasts.

Oh yes, it was all too easy for Raphael to imagine making slow and leisurely love with Beth Blake.

But as the sister of his best friend, and the daughter of the couple who had long ago taken him in as one of their own?

No, Raphael could only ever be the man who stood in silent watch over that woman, who ensured, for her family's sake, that no harm came to her ever again.

BUENOS AIRES
Nights

After dark with Argentina's most infamous billionaires!

Cesar Navarro and Raphael Cordoba—two Argentineans with the wealth, magnetism and ruthlessness to break many a woman's heart….

Grace and Beth—two ordinary British women about to make their first foray into the sultry heat of Buenos Aires nights….

In April 2013 you read all about
Grace and her boss, Cesar, in:

A TASTE OF THE FORBIDDEN

Now read Beth and Raphael's story this month in:

A TOUCH OF NOTORIETY

Carole Mortimer

A TOUCH OF NOTORIETY

BUENOS AIRES
Nights

H HARLEQUIN PRESENTS®

Recycling programs
for this product may
not exist in your area.

ISBN-13: 978-0-373-13145-7

A TOUCH OF NOTORIETY

Copyright © 2013 by Carole Mortimer

Printed in U.S.A.

All about the author...
Carole Mortimer

CAROLE MORTIMER is one of Harlequin's® most popular and prolific authors. Since her first novel, published in 1979, this British writer has shown no signs of slowing her pace. In fact, she has published more than 135 novels!

Her strong, traditional romances, with their distinct style, brilliantly developed characters and romantic plot twists, have earned her an enthusiastic audience worldwide.

Carole was born in a village in England that she claims was so small that "if you blinked as you drove through it, you could miss seeing it completely!" She adds that her parents still live in the house where she first came into the world, and her two brothers live very close by.

Carole's early ambition to become a nurse came to an abrupt end after only one year of training due to a weakness in her back, suffered in the aftermath of a fall. Instead, she went on to work in the computer department of a well-known stationery company.

During her time there, Carole made her first attempt at writing a novel for Harlequin®. "The manuscript was far too short and the plotline not up to standard, so naturally I received a rejection slip," she says. "Not taking rejection well, I went off in a sulk for two years before deciding to 'have another go.'" Her second manuscript was accepted, beginning a long and fruitful career. She says she has "enjoyed every moment of it!"

Carole lives "in a most beautiful part of Britain" with her husband and children.

Other titles by Carole Mortimer available in ebook:

Harlequin Presents®Extra

   129—HIS CHRISTMAS VIRGIN

Harlequin Presents®Extra

   3073—DEFYING DRAKON *(The Lyonedes Legacy)*
   3079—HIS REPUTATION PRECEDES HIM *(The Lyonedes Legacy)*
   3130—A TASTE OF THE FORBIDDEN *(Buenos Aires Nights)*

CHAPTER ONE

'PARDON, SEÑORITA?'

Beth looked up to smile at the handsome young man who, until a few moments ago, had been sitting at a neighbouring table enjoying a cup of coffee at the same outside café in the San Telmo area of Buenos Aires, and shooting her the occasional admiring glance from beautiful chocolate-brown eyes.

But before she could respond she saw a movement out of the corner of her eye as another man approached at a speed totally at odds with his overwhelming height and muscular build. Two seconds later one of the younger man's arms was twisted painfully up behind his back, totally immobilising him.

'Raphael!' Beth muttered in embarrassed protest as she rose to her feet, very tall and slim in a black T-shirt and denims beneath her brown leather jacket.

Raphael didn't so much as glance at her. 'Back off,' he ordered the startled young man coldly, not easing his grip for a second, his expression grimly detached.

'You're the one who should back off, Raphael!' Beth shot him an exasperated glance. 'In fact, you shouldn't even be here...' So much for believing she had managed to escape for even a short time; she should have known that Raphael Cordoba would eventually track her down and ruin her few moments of peace!

'Is this man bothering you?' The young Argentinian braved the other man's wrath as he now spoke to her in heavily accented English.

Was Raphael Cordoba bothering her?

Raphael Cordoba had been 'bothering' Beth since the moment she first met him! And not just because she hated having him dog her footsteps day and night…

Over six feet of male perfection—dark hair framing a chiselled face dominated by piercing blue eyes that any male model would envy, broad shoulders and a leanly muscled body that not even the three-piece suits Raphael habitually wore could disguise—was apt to do that to a woman!

'I thought only to talk to you?' The younger man grimaced, obviously as overwhelmed by the forceful Raphael as Beth was.

'I know.' Beth shot Raphael a censorious glance.

'It is safe to leave you with this man?'

'Safer than with you, you—'

'Raphael, please!' Beth reproved wearily, having to admire the younger man's persistence in the face of Raphael's fierce displeasure. 'It's…complicated,' she excused as she smiled at the other man reassuringly. 'But it's okay—he doesn't have any intention of harming me.'

'You are sure?'

'She is sure,' Raphael answered the younger man grimly, with a deadly expression she was also sure would be in those piercing blue eyes currently hidden behind black mirror-shaded wraparound sunglasses.

And if there was one thing Beth was very sure of, it was that Raphael Cordoba wasn't going to harm her. The opposite, in fact; he was her bodyguard, employed by Cesar Navarro, and here to ensure that no one else harmed her.

Or rather, that no one harmed Gabriela Navarro, the young woman everyone now believed Beth to be.

Except Beth herself…

Just a week ago she had been quietly going about her life in England, enjoying her new job working Monday to Friday in a London publishing house, and feeling only mildly anxious that her sister, Grace, had flown to Argentina for the weekend with her new boss, the breathtakingly handsome billionaire Cesar Navarro, in his private jet. Never in a million years could Beth ever have guessed that Grace's stay in Buenos Aires would have such a profound effect on her own life!

But here she was only days later, also in Buenos Aires, the blood tests having convinced everyone—except Beth herself!—that she was Gabriela, the daughter of Carlos and Esther Navarro, who had been abducted twenty-one years ago.

And Raphael Cordoba, previously Cesar Navarro's own personal bodyguard, now watched over Beth's every move. To the point, it seemed, of attacking handsome young men who had only wanted to talk to her!

'Let him go, Raphael,' Beth muttered wearily, knowing her few minutes of freedom were very definitely over. 'I'm leaving now anyway,' she assured him heavily. 'I think the milk has gone sour in my coffee!' She drew some money from her shoulder bag and threw it down onto the tabletop to cover the cost of her drink before walking off without so much as a second glance at either man. Why bother, when she was never going to be allowed to sit and talk to the younger man—it was safer for him if she didn't—and she knew if she left Raphael would only be a few steps behind her?

As he had been only a few steps behind her in the days since those blood tests had supposedly proven Beth was the missing Gabriela Navarro. Beth clung to that 'supposedly'. She had to. Because she absolutely refused to accept the results of those blood tests until Cesar Navarro's investigations had found some other form of proof to back up that claim.

Much as she had come to like Carlos and Esther Navarro these past few days, Beth was still sure there had to have been some sort of mistake. Her parents—her real parents, James and Carla Lawrence—had loved her. Her adoptive parents, the Blakes, had also loved her. Having to accept that she was neither Elizabeth Lawrence nor Beth Blake, but someone else completely, was enough to make Beth's stomach clench and her hands tremble every time she thought about it.

And, despite her verbal protests, she thought about it a lot...

In the meantime, Cesar Navarro had placed his own bodyguard, Raphael Cordoba, the man who also happened to be Cesar's closest friend, as Beth's shadow.

Cesar Navarro...

Now there, although Beth would never openly admit it, was another man she found totally intimidating.

Another man?

Oh, yes, much as Beth liked to pretend otherwise, she found Raphael Cordoba beyond intimidating. All six feet and several more inches of him. There was a predatory stillness about the man, from the top of his military-short black hair, those piercing blue eyes set in that swarthy and startlingly handsome face, to those wide muscled shoulders and washboard chest, tapered waist, powerful thighs, and down the long, long length of his legs, and all shown to advantage in those expensively tailored suits he always wore.

At thirty-three, Raphael Cordoba looked exactly what he was; ex Argentinian military, and scary as hell!

To complicate matters even further, her sister, Grace, was busy making preparations for her wedding to Cesar Navarro next month. And happy as Beth was for her sister, because even she could see how much Grace loved the handsome Argentinian—a depth of love that was unmistakeably returned by that normally coldly aloof man—it also made Beth feel more trapped than ever, when what she really wanted to do was pack her bags and go back to England and just forget all of the Navarro family existed.

Which was never going to happen. Even if Beth could have made good her escape, she couldn't escape Grace's engagement and future marriage to Cesar Navarro. And no matter how much Beth might believe she was and only ever had been Elizabeth Lawrence before being adopted by the Blakes, she could never hurt Carlos and Esther Navarro by disappearing—as their baby daughter had twenty-one years ago—in that cruel way.

Fortunately she didn't have to allow for that concern in regard to hurting Raphael Cordoba's feelings! 'Will you just back off?' she snapped at him now as she sensed him walking—striding with that predatory grace that was such an inborn part of him—close behind her.

Instead he fell into step beside her. 'It was very foolish of you to disappear from Cesar's apartment in that thoughtless way.'

Beth winced at the rebuke. 'I felt as if I was slowly being suffocated!'

Raphael's mouth tightened. 'You still should not have worried Esther in that way.'

How did he do that? How did Raphael know exactly the right thing to say to make Beth feel guilty?

Because impossible, unbearable, as her current situation was for her, Beth didn't want to hurt the couple who had already suffered so much. To the extent that once Cesar

was old enough to go to university, and despite their love
for each other, Esther and Carlos had no longer been able
to live together with the ghost of their beloved baby daughter standing so painfully between them.

A beloved daughter the couple now sincerely believed
to have been returned to them in Beth…

It was a belief Beth simply didn't—couldn't—accept.

Not least because, at almost twenty-four, she felt like a
fish out of water in the opulent lifestyle the Navarros all
enjoyed so naturally. And while she had grown fond of
the two older Navarros these past few days, and enjoyed
nothing more than challenging Cesar Navarro's haughty
arrogance, she innately knew she didn't really belong here.
With the Navarro family. Or in Argentina itself. She was
English through and through, and comfortable in her own
skin, as a product of her well-off but far from wealthy
adoptive parents, Clive and Heather Blake.

Nevertheless, Beth was totally aware—as was Raphael!—of the effect the supposed return of their daughter had had on the older Navarros' relationship. After years
of living apart, Carlos in Buenos Aires and Esther in the
US where she grew up, the couple had been sharing a bedroom in Cesar's apartment since Grace had returned to
Buenos Aires with Beth at her side…

Beth sighed heavily. 'I'm sorry, okay? I just needed
some time to myself.'

Raphael looked down at Beth Blake from behind the
mirrored shades of his sunglasses, easily able to read the
emotions flitting across her expressive—and extremely
beautiful—face. A part of him even sympathised with
her obvious bewilderment at being taken to be the newly
returned Gabriela Navarro. But the medical proof of
blood tests could not be easily denied, and, as a childhood friend of Cesar's, Raphael knew how important this

young woman was to the Navarro family. A family—the calm and steady Carlos, the warm and loving Esther, and the coolly arrogant Cesar—who had taken Raphael in as one of their own after a row with his father so many years ago had caused him to leave home.

As such, whether the feisty and stubbornly independent Beth Blake accepted her new identity or not—and she obviously did not—Raphael intended ensuring, by whatever means possible, that she remained safe while on his watch. And, as far as Beth was concerned, his watch now covered the whole twenty-four hours of every one of her days!

Something she had shown him—once again!—by just disappearing from Cesar's apartment earlier that she deeply resented. 'Gabriela—'

'My name is Beth, damn it!' she corrected, her eyes flashing darkly, two bright spots of angry colour having appeared in her cheeks.

Cheeks normally as pale and smooth as the finest porcelain, her eyes a deep rich brown above her small uptilting nose, her mouth a perfect bow above her stubbornly determined chin. As for her long silky hair...! Raphael had only ever seen one other woman with hair those heavy layers of all shades of blond, from gold to the palest silver, and that was Esther Navarro. The woman blood tests had shown to be Beth's birth mother.

He shrugged broad shoulders. 'I now think of you as Gabriela Navarro.' Having been only a precocious two years old when she was taken from her real family, Beth would no more remember having met Raphael before than she did the Navarro family. But he remembered her, had stayed often with Cesar's family even then, usually during the school holidays, and Gabriela had been Cesar's beloved baby sister, a golden-haired angel to be petted and spoilt by the two much older boys.

At the moment Beth Blake looked as pettable as a spitting tigress. 'Well, isn't it just lucky for me that I have absolutely no interest in what, or who, *you* happen to think I am!'

'I do not "happen" to think anything, it has been medically proven as fact that you are Gabriela Navarro. And it is equally lucky for me that I have absolutely no interest in what you may think of me, either.' Raphael allowed a mocking smile to quirk his lips, knowing by the way those rich brown eyes narrowed that Beth Blake did not appreciate his humour at her expense.

She gave an inelegant snort. 'You really don't want to know what I think of you, Raphael!'

As her bodyguard, perhaps not, but as a man? Oh, yes, much as she might wish it were otherwise, the completely carnal glances Beth Blake gave him from beneath those thick dark lashes whenever she thought Raphael wasn't looking at her told him that she saw him very much as a man. And was attracted to what she saw.

As much as she resented his status as her bodyguard!

A status that Raphael, equally aware of the allure of the fullness of Beth's breasts and the sensual curve of her gently swaying hips, was determined to keep front and centre in all of his dealings with Beth Blake. To do anything else would compromise his protection of her.

'Perhaps not,' he drawled dismissively. 'Shall we return to the apartment now?'

She shot him a weary glance. 'Why do you bother asking, when you have every intention of taking me back there now whether I want to go or not?'

'And why do you bother continually fighting what is, after all, your destiny?' Raphael eyed her coolly from behind those wraparound sunglasses.

Beth gave a pained frown. 'Perhaps because I don't see it as my destiny?'

'Grace appears to be having little difficulty in accepting the Navarro family as her own.'

Beth Blake gave a rueful smile. 'It's different for Grace. She's chosen to fall in love with Cesar, to accept Cesar's marriage proposal, and to become a member of the Navarro family and all that entails.'

Raphael arched dark brows. 'Does anyone choose to fall in love?' As Cesar's personal bodyguard until a few days ago, Raphael had been a silent witness to the other couple falling in love, and he did not believe it to have been in the least as smooth and pleasant as Beth's words implied that it was.

Perhaps it was now that Cesar and Grace had acknowledged their love for each other and were planning their wedding, but certainly not initially, when the sparks had flown and they had argued about almost everything except the attraction building so rapidly between them.

Much as he and Beth now argued about everything...

No, it was not the same at all, Raphael dismissed determinedly. Much as he might be attracted to Beth Blake's fiery nature and her beauty, and the supple and desirable curves of her slender body, where she was concerned Raphael had no intention of allowing that attraction to become anything more than visual appreciation. She was Cesar's beloved little sister returned to him, and as such Beth could never become one of the numerous women who had fleetingly shared Raphael's bed these last fifteen years.

Which were the only relationships with women Raphael allowed in his life, having learnt of a woman's treachery at a young age, from his own father's second wife.

'Probably not.' Beth gave a grimace as she answered

him. 'But Grace at least has her love for Cesar as reason to try and embrace his lifestyle.'

'And you do not have love for Cesar, and your parents, as a reason to try and do the same?'

It was impossible for Beth to miss the censure in Raphael Cordoba's tone. And no doubt, if she took off those damned sunglasses of his, she would find that same censure in those piercing blue eyes. 'Stop twisting my words, Raphael,' she murmured instead. 'And how can I possibly love three people I didn't even know existed a couple of weeks ago?' And there, in the proverbial nutshell, was the reason for Beth's feeling at a loss as to how to deal with this situation.

She wished she could remember Carlos and Esther as having once been her parents, even the arrogant Cesar as having been her brother, but the truth of the matter was that Beth had absolutely no recollection of any of them. Furthering her belief that she couldn't possibly be related to them, no matter what those blood tests said to the contrary.

Time would take care of that, the two older Navarros had assured her, together and individually. Time they obviously expected Beth to spend here in Argentina getting to know all of them...

'Not a day has gone by this past twenty-one years when they have not all thought of you.' Obviously Raphael Cordoba didn't feel the same degree of patience towards her in that regard. Or any patience at all, judging by the coldness of his expression as he looked down the length of his arrogant nose at her.

Beth sighed heavily. 'And I'm sincerely sorry for that. But only in the way any third party would feel after hearing of the abduction of the Navarros' baby daughter, and the heartache they have suffered in the years since,' she added firmly.

His jaw tightened. 'You do not consider that Carlos and Esther have already suffered enough heartbreak on your behalf?'

'That's hardly fair—'

'They are also two of the kindest, warmest people I have ever known.'

'I'm sure they are.' Beth looked pained. 'But I've already had, and loved, two sets of parents. A third one not only seems unlikely but…well, excessive.'

Raphael's eyes narrowed. 'The difference is that they are your natural parents—'

'Why is it that none of you will even try to understand why I just can't accept that?' Her own eyes darkened almost to the same black as Cesar's when he was angry or upset. 'Why I can't accept any of this? And why I have to go back to England,' she added determinedly.

'Everyone *is* trying—' He bit back the steely rebuke he had been about to deliver as he instead straightened his shoulders determinedly; arguing with the person he was employed to protect was not conducive to building the trust between them that was necessary in such situations. A trust Beth Blake stubbornly refused to give him. This was something he would need to speak to Cesar about when they were able to speak privately together. 'If you will not stay in Argentina for the Navarros' sake, you might at least consider it for Grace's. She is, after all, arranging her wedding next month to Cesar.'

'Ooh, low blow, Raphael,' Beth murmured dryly. 'If all else fails bring in the sister angle.'

He gave an unapologetic grin. 'Is it working?'

'Of course,' she acknowledged heavily.

Raphael didn't enjoy seeing the dejected look on that beautiful face. 'If it is any consolation, Grace argued constantly with Cesar, too, when they first met.'

Beth raised blond brows over surprised brown eyes. 'Your point being?'

She looked so much like her older brother at that moment that Raphael had trouble holding back his derisive laughter at Beth's continued insistence that she couldn't possibly be related to the Navárro family. At this moment she was undoubtedly every inch a Navarro!

'My point being that the Navarro family cannot be all bad if Grace has learnt to love them in such a short time,' he drawled dryly.

Beth tilted her head as she gazed up at him quizzically for several seconds. 'You like my big sister...' she finally murmured slowly.

'I do, yes,' Raphael confirmed without hesitation. Grace Blake was as feisty and outspoken as her younger adopted sister, and was without a doubt the perfect match for the often remote and arrogant Cesar.

Beth gave a derisive smile. 'Then perhaps there's hope for you yet, Raphael!'

He arched dark brows. 'In what regard?'

'In regard to your belonging to the human race, after all, rather than the unemotional robot I had thought you to be!' she retorted.

Raphael drew in a hissing breath at the deliberate insult. 'You will go too far, Gabriela!'

'And then what?' Beth chose to ignore his no doubt deliberate use of that name. This time...

'Then I might have reason to prove to you just how much of a robot I am not!'

Beth looked up at him searchingly, wishing—not for the first time today—that his piercing blue eyes weren't hidden behind those damned sunglasses. Although perhaps not—no doubt his gaze would be as razor-sharp as his tone...

'Is that supposed to scare me?' she prompted lightly.

It was now possible to feel the laser-sharpness of his gaze through those protective shades. 'There are far more…enjoyable ways of subduing a disobedient woman than scaring her,' he drawled softly.

Beth felt a shiver of reaction down the length of her spine. Not of fear, but of arousal…

Which was the real reason she constantly felt the need to challenge this man, of course. She had never been so physically aware of another man in the way she was of Raphael Cordoba. Of those arrogant good looks. And the sheer power of that muscled body beneath those perfectly tailored designer suits. Even the way Raphael smelt, sandalwood and lemon and pure healthy male, was enough to put all of her senses on alert. So much so that Beth was usually aware of his presence in a room before she even saw him. It was *not* a comfortable feeling for a woman who had believed, until she met this arrogant Argentinian, that she was cool and sophisticated when it came to her reaction to men.

Hot and bothered more accurately described her reaction to Raphael Cordoba!

'"Subduing a disobedient woman"?' Beth gave him a derisive glance. 'Do you have to behave quite so much the Neanderthal?'

He gave a tight, humourless smile. 'I assure you, no woman has ever had reason to complain about my…methods of securing their submission.'

Beth would just bet they hadn't! The man was sexual seduction on two long sexy legs, so what was there to complain about?

Plenty, when Beth really didn't want to hear about the other women Raphael had been involved with.

'Then more fool them,' she snapped disgustedly before

turning on her heel and striding off in the direction of Cesar's apartment.

All the time aware of Raphael as he continued to follow two steps behind her.

Just as she was also aware, by the tingling sensation quivering down the length of her spine, that those piercing blue eyes were now levelled intently on the gentle sway of her denim-clad hips and backside as she walked in front of him...

CHAPTER TWO

'OH BUT—'

'I think we should let Gab—Beth go back to England if that is what she wishes to do,' Cesar gently interrupted his mother as she would have voiced her protest to Beth's reminder that she was due to fly home tomorrow.

He surprised Beth with that support; she had felt sure that the arrogant Cesar would be just as opposed to the idea of her going back to England tomorrow as his parents obviously were. Maybe Grace's more reasonable attitude was having a beneficial influence on the man, after all!

Beth smiled her gratitude across the luncheon table at him. 'Thank you, Cesar.'

He nodded. 'Raphael will accompany you, of course.'

A premature gratitude, obviously! 'I don't think so—'

'And I will arrange for you to fly back in the private jet—'

'Stop right there, Cesar!' Beth bristled just at the mention of bodyguards and private jets. An indignation that only deepened she saw the mocking smile curving Raphael Cordoba's chiselled mouth as he appeared to be on watchful guard outside in the hallway—while obviously listening to their conversation. 'I have a perfectly good return ticket booked on the commercial flight back to England tomorrow—'

'Carlos…!' A distressed Esther looked at her husband appealingly.

'Perhaps it might be better if you were to accept Cesar's offer,' Carlos Navarro reasoned gently.

'I'm sorry, but I'm really not comfortable doing that.' Beth grimaced apologetically. 'And I certainly don't want or need Raphael to accompany me anywhere—'

'Be reasonable, Beth…' Grace interrupted quietly but firmly even as she touched Beth's hand cajolingly.

'I am being reasonable.' Beth knew that she sounded, and no doubt appeared, childishly mulish rather than reasonable. 'No one else but the people seated around this table—and Raphael—' she shot him an impatient glance as she saw that mocking smile had now become a smirk '—is even aware that you all think I'm Gabriela—'

'We *know* that you are, honey.' Esther smiled across at her warmly.

Beth swallowed down the emotional lump that had formed in her throat at the unconditional love she saw shining in the older woman's eyes. 'Yes. Well. As you know, I still have difficulty accepting that.' She avoided meeting any of their gazes as she stared down at the dining table, totally unable to deal with the hope she knew was shining in Carlos's and Esther's eyes, the censure in Cesar's, the understanding in Grace's, let alone the mockery she knew she would see in Raphael's piercing blue eyes now that he was no longer wearing those dark glasses. 'Until Cesar can supply me with further proof, I'm still Beth Blake as far as I'm concerned. And Beth Blake has a home and a job in England to go back to,' she added firmly.

Cesar scowled darkly. 'I assumed when you said you wished to go back to England that it was only so that you might close up the house there and deal with any other affairs—such as resigning from your place of work—before flying back here.'

'Why on earth would you have assumed that?' Beth gave a pained frown. 'I worked hard to get my degree, and I love my job, so why would I want to give that up?'

'Possibly because you are Gabriela Navarro, and as such have no reason to work?' Cesar grated harshly.

'Even if you do prove beyond a shadow of a doubt that I'm Gabriela—'

'We already have.'

'I will still refuse to sit around here like some pampered poodle—' Beth broke off as she heard a snort of what she was sure was laughter from the direction of the hallway. Nor was she convinced otherwise by the bland expression on Raphael Cordoba's face when she gave him a long, suspicious glance before turning slowly back to frown at Cesar. 'I wasn't brought up to sit around painting my toenails—'

'Oh, I feel sure a "pampered poodle" would pay someone else to paint their toenails,' Cesar snapped.

'You aren't helping the situation, Cesar,' Grace cut in with soft reproof.

His expression softened as he smiled down at the woman he loved. But that smile faded as he turned back to Beth. 'I am sure that Grace would rather you remained here and helped her with the arrangements for the wedding.'

'Raphael already tried the sister approach,' Beth told him wearily.

'And?'

'And of course I'll come back for the wedding; I am the chief bridesmaid, after all. But, in the meantime, Grace has Esther to help with those arrangements.' The latter was an argument she knew Cesar had no answer to. His mother was in her element with the arrangements for his wedding to Grace. 'Which leaves me free to return to my life and job in England until a few days before the wedding.'

Cesar breathed impatiently down his nose. 'Perhaps we might…compromise, in that you agree to take a month's leave of absence from your place of work to come back here—'

'A month's leave of absence?' Beth repeated incredulously as she sat up straighter in her chair. 'Asking for this week's holiday just after I had started working there didn't exactly go down well!'

Cesar's mouth firmed stubbornly. 'Then perhaps I should consider buying the company, in which case my first instruction as the new head of that company would be for you to take a month's leave of absence.'

Beth only wished that he were joking, or at least being sarcastic, but, as she was only too well aware, Cesar was as rich if not richer than several small countries, and so perfectly capable of doing exactly as he said he would.

She turned to give Grace a disbelieving shake of her head. 'And you're actually thinking of marrying this megalomaniac!'

Grace gave a husky laugh. 'I most certainly am. Don't worry.' She gave Beth's hand another conciliatory pat. 'He improves with acquaintance!'

This time there was no mistaking the sound of Raphael's throaty chuckle. Beth turned to look at him challengingly. 'Perhaps you should come in here and join us if you have something to add to this conversation?'

Raphael eyed her mockingly. 'I am merely an employee…'

This time it was Beth who snorted. 'I think we both know that, as a long-term friend of Cesar, and head of his security worldwide, you aren't "merely" an anything! Besides which,' she continued firmly as Raphael would have spoken, 'as this conversation has revealed that you're expected to come to England with me, it would seem to concern you as much as it does me...' she added with a frown.

'Yes, come in and join us for coffee, Raphael,' Cesar invited smoothly before turning to request another cup as Maria brought in the tray of coffee things.

Raphael had found time to speak to the other man before lunch, in regard to Beth's resentment of having him as her bodyguard, a concern that Cesar had dismissed by assuring him, whether Beth liked it or not, there was no one else to whom Cesar would entrust his sister's safety. And Cesar knew firsthand just how stubborn the Blake women could be; Grace and Beth might both be adopted, and from completely different parents, but their stubbornness of character was undeniably similar!

'Please do join us, Raphael.' Esther turned to smile at him warmly as she poured the coffee for all of them once Maria had returned with the sixth cup. 'With all that's happened this last few days I haven't had chance to ask how your family are,' she prompted gently as Raphael strode into the dining room.

All that had happened these last few days had included Esther's own stay in hospital after a car crash in which she had thankfully only received a blow to the head and bruising. She was now fully recovered, but the incident had quickly been followed by the shock of having Gabriela return to them in the guise of Beth Blake. Both were reason enough for her not to have found the opportunity to enquire after the family Raphael usually managed to avoid seeing whenever he was in Argentina!

'All well, the last time I asked, thank you,' he dismissed lightly as he folded his length down onto the seat a smiling Carlos had pushed back for him.

'Does your family live in Buenos Aires?' Beth's curiosity obviously got the better of her.

Raphael met her gaze coolly. 'No.'

'Then where—?'

'I believe we were discussing the arrangements for your return to England,' Cesar cut in decisively.

Beth continued to look at the bland-faced Raphael for several minutes longer, sensing some sort of schism in regard to his own family, a schism the Navarro family seemed well aware of. Not that anyone was going to explain that to her any time soon, if Raphael's closed expression was any indication. 'No, you were discussing it.' She turned back to Cesar. 'I've already stated what my own arrangements are.'

'Those arrangements are unacceptable,' the man who would shortly be her brother-in-law—if not her actual brother!—dismissed with his usual arrogance.

'Not to me.'

'Beth, try to understand how Cesar and your— His parents feel,' Grace encouraged softly. 'They've already lost Gabriela once,' she added.

Beth felt what was becoming a familiar sinking sensation in the pit of her stomach.

Having no children of her own yet—never having come even close to being involved in a serious relationship, let alone thought of having children!—Beth found it hard to completely relate to the tragedy of having a child abducted when she was only two years old, followed by twenty-one years of not knowing what had become of her.

It became even more of a nightmare when she considered that the Navarros so obviously believed she was that child returned to them!

And no matter what Cesar and Raphael might think to the contrary, she really did like Carlos and Esther, and had no wish to hurt them any more than they had already been hurt over the loss of their young daughter...

She sighed. 'Okay, I'll agree to fly back in the private jet.' She grimaced. 'I'll even agree to having Raphael accompany me— Don't say a word,' she warned hardly as he raised mocking brows. 'But I draw the line at taking a leave of absence from my job—and if you dare to buy the company, Cesar, I will simply hand in my notice and go elsewhere,' she warned firmly as he would have spoken.

'At which time I will simply buy whichever company you seek employment with next,' he stated mildly.

'You really are a control freak.'

'And you are as stubborn as a mule!'

'Hah, it takes one to know one!'

'I see now, Grace, why you came to the initial conclusion that Cesar and Beth may be related,' Raphael spoke mildly. 'Even without the proof of the blood tests, it is possible to see that the two of you are brother and sister,' he explained as he found himself the focus of two pairs of identical chocolate-brown eyes, the one coolly questioning, the other accusing.

Grace chuckled softly. 'It is pretty noticeable, isn't it?'

'Oh, yes!' Raphael confirmed with feeling.

'Everyone's a comedian!' Beth threw her hands up in disgust.

Raphael grinned, unabashed. 'No doubt the situation is more amusing looked at from the outside.'

'No doubt it is,' Beth acknowledged dryly. 'So, where were we? Oh, yes.' She turned back to Cesar. 'I've agreed, as the sister of your future wife, to the private jet, and having Raphael see that I'm safely delivered back to England, so now it's your turn to agree to your half of the bargain and let me get on with the career I've worked so hard for.'

Raphael looked at Beth appreciatively; she was approaching this situation from a business angle Cesar could and would relate to. The only problem with these particular negotiations was that Cesar never compromised when it came to the welfare of the people who mattered to him. Stubbornly independent as Beth might be—and in denial as to her true identity—Cesar firmly believed her to be the sister he had adored when she was a baby, and for whom he and his parents had mourned these past twenty-one years.

Although none of them could possibly have realised that Gabriela would one day be returned to them a fully grown and independent young woman who refused to accept her heritage!

Cesar sat forward to take his coffee cup from his mother. 'I do not believe you understood my earlier remark correctly. Raphael will not only accompany you back to England, but remain there for as long as you do.'

'What?' Beth gasped incredulously. 'Not only is that utterly ridiculous, it's also impractical!'

'Nevertheless, that is my compromise.' Cesar remained stubbornly decisive.

Beth turned to look at Raphael impatiently. 'And you're happy with that, are you?'

His eyes narrowed. 'I go wherever Cesar wishes me to go.'

'Oh, wonderful!' She gave a disgusted shake of her head. 'And exactly where do you intend staying while you're there? Because you certainly aren't staying in my home with me!'

Raphael eyed her coolly. 'Hopefully I will have things in place before we leave tomorrow.'

She eyed him warily. 'What things?'

Raphael maintained a blandly unsmiling expression as he held back his inner amusement at Beth's obvious suspicion. 'Things.'

'Grace, do something!' She turned to appeal to her older sister.

'Darling, I know this is difficult for you, but—' Grace winced '—in the circumstances—' she glanced at Esther and Carlos '—I have to agree with Cesar and Raphael.'

'Unbelievable!' Beth stood up noisily from the table. 'By all means, Cesar, you and Raphael arrogantly go ahead and finish making your arrangements—personally, I intend to go and start packing,' she muttered emotionally. 'The sooner I'm out of here, the better!' She rushed out of the dining room.

'She doesn't mean it, Esther.' Grace sat forward to reassure her future mother-in-law as the other woman paled. 'Beth's upset, and a little disorientated by all the changes being asked of her.'

'She is spoilt and willful.' A nerve pulsed in Cesar's rigidly clenched jaw as a door was heard slamming down the hallway. Beth's bedroom door, no doubt.

'She is frightened,' Raphael corrected softly, his gaze still turned in the direction in which Beth had just departed as he rose slowly to his feet. 'Will you allow me to go and talk to her?'

'Would you?' Grace turned to him gratefully. 'I would go myself, but at the moment Beth seems to see me as having defected to—' She broke off with an uncomfortable grimace.

'The enemy,' Esther finished for her sadly.

'No, not the enemy,' Grace assured her instantly. 'Try to understand this from Beth's point of view,' she continued gently. 'Not only has she lost two sets of parents already, but she's lived the past twenty-one years of her life in complete ignorance of all of you, and it's going to take time, and patience on your part—' she gave Cesar a pointed look '—for her to accept exactly who she really is.'

And, in the meantime, for all that Raphael understood and sympathised with Beth's confusion of emotions, it was time for her to start considering feelings other than her own. 'If you will all excuse me,' he muttered with grim distraction before striding purposefully from the room.

Beth refused to cry as she threw her clothes into the open suitcase she had tossed on top of her bed a few minutes ago.

How and when had her life become such a nightmare? Including all of her carefully made plans for a future in publishing?

The moment Grace had met Cesar Navarro's parents just over a week ago, that was when. And Beth refused to—

'If you were my sister—newly returned to me or otherwise—I would have put you over my knee and soundly spanked your spoilt little backside by now!'

She hastily blinked back all evidence of tears before turning sharply to face Raphael, her spine straightening determinedly as he stood overwhelmingly tall and wide in the now open doorway. 'Then it's just as well I'm not your sister, isn't it?' she snapped.

Those laser-blue eyes narrowed in warning. 'You hurt Esther just now, and that is as unforgivable to me as it is to Cesar and Carlos.' The steely edge to his tone was unmistakeable.

Beth eyed him warily. 'I didn't mean to hurt Esther...'

'And yet you did.'

Her gaze dropped guiltily from his. 'I'll apologise to her before I leave.'

He sighed heavily. 'As I said earlier, why do you continue to fight what is inevitable?'

Her eyes flashed darkly. 'And as I answered earlier—because to me it isn't inevitable!'

Raphael gave an impatient shake of his head. 'You are a fool if you believe that. Even more so if you think Cesar will ever leave you, his sister Gabriela, in a position of vulnerability ever again for even a moment! The fact that the Navarros are allowing you to leave at all—'

'No one is "allowing" me to do anything.'

'But they are,' Raphael corrected harshly. 'You think that Esther could not stop you if she were determined to do so? That she could not break down and cry, beg you not to leave them, and so make you feel too guilty to go?'

Beth flinched. 'Esther is far too dignified to ever behave in that way.'

'Yes, she is,' he acknowledged softly. 'But you are the daughter she has grieved for for over twenty years. Letting you go now is like having her mother's heart ripped out for a second time.'

Beth blinked. 'Then why doesn't she try to stop me?'

He shrugged. 'I can only believe it is because she knows it is best to let you go, and simply hope that one day you will choose to come back.'

'And if I don't?'

'You will.'

'You sound very sure of that.'

'Yes,' he replied abruptly.

Beth sighed deeply. 'You're so obviously of the opinion that I should just accept all of this—'

'I think you should accept what is,' Raphael corrected harshly. 'And that the sooner you do so, the easier this situation will become for you.'

'I didn't ask for any of this—this mess.'

'Neither did your mother, father, or brother!'

Her cheeks flushed. 'They aren't—'

'But they are, Beth,' he insisted softly.

She shook her head. 'I simply can't—I won't accept that, not until Cesar comes up with more conclusive proof.'

'The blood tests are conclusive proof.'

'Not to me!'

Raphael sighed. 'What would it take to convince you?'

'I have absolutely no idea.' She sighed wearily.

'Perhaps a headstone in a graveyard with the name Elizabeth Lawrence, aged two, engraved on it?'

Beth raised her head slowly to look at him, her face paling even as her breath caught in her throat as she could read nothing from Raphael's closed expression. 'Are you saying that such a headstone exists?'

He shrugged those broad shoulders. 'Would it help to convince you if it did?'

The palms of her hands felt clammy just at thoughts of that tiny grave with its damning headstone. 'Do you already have the proof that Elizabeth Lawrence died?'

'Not yet, no,' Raphael admitted reluctantly.

'But you will have?'

His mouth firmed. 'Possibly.'

Beth stared at him wordlessly for several moments, unable to look away from those piercing blue eyes. 'You aren't just coming to England to act as my bodyguard, are you?' she realised dully.

He gave a slight smile. 'Did you ever believe that I was?'

Had she? In her heart of hearts, had Beth really thought that Cesar would ever give up trying to prove she was his sister Gabriela? And that he wouldn't take full advantage of Raphael's presence in England to continue those investigations.

'And if you find that proof?'

Raphael shrugged. 'Then perhaps you will finally be convinced.'

Would she? Was it really possible the original Elizabeth Lawrence had died? And if so, where was she buried?

It had only been a matter of a few days since Grace had put forward the suggestion that Beth might be the Navarros' missing daughter, and those blood tests had convinced the Navarros, if not Beth, that she was. But they had also been days when she knew Cesar was continuing his own investigations, looking for the truth of how Gabriela could have been taken from Argentina to England twenty-one years ago, and given the identity of Elizabeth Lawrence…

'There are many of us who, given a choice, would have preferred to have been born into a family which is not their own,' Raphael drawled as he saw the array of emotions flickering across Beth's expressive face. Dismay being the last of them.

'Even you?'

His jaw tightened. 'We were not talking about me.'

'Weren't we?'

'No,' Raphael replied with finality. His family, and the reason for the years of estrangement from his father, was not a subject he wished to talk about. The same reason that Raphael preferred to keep his relationships with women to the physical rather than the emotional. A line Beth Blake deliberately stepped over almost every time the two of them were together…

'And if—if you find there is such a grave, are you going to tell me about it first or just report straight to Cesar?' She looked at him challengingly.

His mouth thinned. 'I am employed by Cesar—'

'Please, Raphael!' She looked up at him appealingly.

Raphael frowned darkly as he knew he was not as immune to that appeal as he might have wished. 'Shall we just wait and see what happens?'

'You sound as if you're placating a child!'

'Then perhaps you should stop acting like one.' Raphael bit out his frustration with this situation. With the fact that he had never regarded Beth as a child.

Oh, she was almost ten years younger than him, and outspoken in a way he had never encountered before—except perhaps from her adopted sister, Grace—but there was no doubting Beth's womanly curves, or her kissable mouth, or that Raphael's response to those curves and those sensual lips was purely male!

She gave a pained frown now before turning away. 'If you wouldn't mind leaving now, I need to finish packing.'

'And if I do mind?'

Beth stilled, as she knew, by the closeness of Raphael's voice, that he was now standing just behind her. So close that she could feel the heat of his body and smell the spicy allure of his cologne, and that pure male smell that was Raphael alone. An insidious and heady combination, along with the predatory power of the man himself, that Beth responded to in spite of herself...

'Beth?'

She kept her expression deliberately cool as she turned to face him, that coolness wavering slightly as she found that Raphael was standing only inches away from her, those piercing blue eyes still narrowed in his harshly chiselled face as he looked down the length of his nose at her.

Beth's chin rose determinedly in the face of that implacability.

'I've agreed to go back to England in Cesar's jet, and to having you accompany me. Isn't that enough?'

'For now, perhaps...'

Her eyes flashed darkly. 'What more do any of you want from me?'

What did Raphael want from this woman?

From Beth Blake, a woman he could not deny that he found physically attractive?

It was all too easy to imagine making love with that woman; kissing those delectable and poutingly stubborn lips, enjoying and pleasuring those lean and silkily slender curves, caressing and tasting the fullness of her breasts, arousing her until she was wet and open to his sinking his shaft between those delicious thighs, slowly and torturously at first, and then faster, pumping into her until they both found release.

Oh, yes, it was all too easy for Raphael to imagine making slow and leisurely love with Beth Blake.

But as Gabriela Navarro, the woman who was the sister of his best friend, and the daughter of the couple who had long ago taken him in as one of their own?

No, Raphael could only ever be the man who stood in silent watch over that woman, who ensured, for her family's sake, that no harm came to her ever again.

His mouth tightened. 'I do not recall ever saying that I want or need anything from you.'

She blinked at the harshness of his tone. 'Please don't hold back, Raphael. Just say it like it is!' she scorned.

He raised cool brows. 'I thought that was what I was doing.'

She raised her eyes heavenwards. 'I was being sarcastic!'

'I am well aware of that.' He nodded. 'I have also noticed that you resort to that sarcasm whenever you are feeling defensive.'

Her eyes widened indignantly. 'Why on earth should I be feeling defensive?'

Raphael shrugged. 'You would have to tell me that.'

Beth looked up at him wordlessly for several long, searching, seconds. 'No, I don't think I have anything else to say to you right now,' she finally said slowly. 'And surely you have those other "things" you need to go off and organise before we leave tomorrow?' she added with hard dismissal.

He allowed a slight smile to curve his lips. 'I do, yes.'

'Well, don't let me keep you,' she prompted tautly as Raphael still made no effort to leave her bedroom.

Raphael continued to hold that challenging brown gaze with his own as he fought that inner battle not to take Beth in his arms and kiss that smart mouth of hers until she was senseless and wanting in his arms.

To *enjoy* kissing that sarcastic mouth of hers until she was senseless and wanting!

The problem with that, of course, was that he might just enjoy kissing Beth a little too much. So much that he would not want to stop at just kissing her…

He gave a terse nod of his head as he stepped away from her. 'I am sure that Cesar will keep you informed as to what time we are to leave tomorrow.'

'Oh, I'm sure he will, too,' she replied dryly.

He frowned his irritation. 'His only concern is your protection.'

'And what's your concern, Raphael?' She eyed him mockingly.

His mouth thinned. 'Cesar does not employ me to have concerns, only solutions to security problems.'

'Then it's probably time you went away and found some!' Having delivered her final scathing comment, Beth turned away, knowing she was wasting her time trying to bait this man. Raphael Cordoba really was that robot she had accused him of being earlier.

Nevertheless, she breathed a heavy sigh of relief as she heard his predatory step crossing the bedroom seconds later before the door closed softly behind him.

She dropped down weakly onto the side of the bed, her bravado of a few minutes ago completely evaporating as she once again acknowledged that, unless evidence could be found to the contrary, proving once and for all that she *wasn't* Gabriela Navarro, her life was never, ever going to be the same again.

CHAPTER THREE

'COMFORTABLE?'

Beth turned to look at Raphael Cordoba as he sat beside the chauffeur in the front of the car driving them from the airport to the home in London she had once shared with her whole family and now shared only with Grace—*had* shared with Grace, because, once her sister was married to Cesar, Beth knew Grace would never live in that family home with her again.

Which, besides being sad, meant that the house was going to be far too big for Beth to live in on her own. Maybe she could advertise for someone to share it with her—

'Gabriela?'

Beth ground her teeth together at Raphael's deliberate use of the name she refused to recognise as being her own. And it had been deliberate, she was sure. 'Yes, I'm very comfortable, thank you,' she assured him with cool politeness. The same cool politeness that had existed between the two of them since Beth said her goodbyes to Grace and the Navarro family the previous evening before leaving for the airport with Raphael.

Beth frowned slightly as she remembered they had been tearful goodbyes on the part of Grace and Esther, stoic but warm on Carlos's, and slightly disapproving on Cesar's...

Although Beth had learnt there were definite advantages to those chauffeur-driven limousines and private jets she had previously pooh-poohed at! No long wait at the airport before boarding the flight for one thing, the limousine having driven them straight to the plane, and the aircraft taking off only minutes after she and Raphael had stepped aboard. There had also been a bedroom at the back of the plane, which Beth had definitely enjoyed. Not only had it meant she could sleep for much of the flight back, but it had also meant she'd had somewhere to escape to when she'd had enough of Raphael's brooding silence. There hadn't been the long wait beside the carousel for the baggage to arrive, either, once they landed in London, as the bags were instead loaded straight into the boot of another chauffeur-driven limousine waiting for them on the tarmac.

The English weather wasn't too welcoming, though. Heavy rain was falling as they stepped out of the plane, causing Raphael to grimace with displeasure as he held an umbrella over Beth until she had descended the steps and climbed into the back of the limousine. He put down the umbrella and climbed into the passenger seat beside the chauffeur, drawing up a definite line of demarcation: he was the employee, and Beth was the younger sister of his employer.

He needn't have bothered; Beth was all too aware of the fact that, as far as Raphael was concerned, she was just another part of his job.

And did that bother her?

Of course it didn't, Beth told herself firmly. Raphael Cordoba might be dark and brooding, and handsome as sin, but he was also rude and arrogant, and totally disapproving of her, and the sooner he returned to Argentina, the better Beth would like it—

Was she protesting just a little too much?

There was no doubting that Raphael was older, more sophisticated, and just plain more dangerous than any of the men Beth had been attracted to in the past. And she didn't usually find dark and brooding in the least interesting, either. Or rude and arrogant. And yet...

Much as she might want to deny it, Beth knew she had been aware of Raphael since the moment she first met him, and there had been a definite frisson of physical awareness when she and Raphael had been alone together in her bedroom two days ago. The sort of awareness that had sent a shiver down her spine, causing her nipples to tingle, and between her thighs to feel warm.

Sexual attraction.

She was sexually attracted to Raphael, in a way she never had been with any of the men she had actually been out on dates with.

Or maybe it was just that she saw his disapproval of her as a challenge?

Beth studied Raphael's profile now as he talked softly with the chauffeur, a strong and chiselled profile: high cheekbones, a long and aristocratic nose, sculptured lips, and a strong square jaw that at the moment was in need of a shave. He was once again wearing one of those perfectly tailored three-piece suits—charcoal today, with a white silk shirt and meticulously knotted blue tie that matched the cerulean blue of his eyes, and yet those expensive trappings of sophistication did absolutely nothing to detract from the leashed power of his lean and muscled body, as if he were coiled and ready to spring at a moment's notice. Which, no doubt, he was...

Beth felt that familiar shiver course down the length of her spine as she watched him beneath lowered lashes, her nipples tightening, the fit of her denims suddenly feeling uncomfortably tight against the swollen folds between her thighs.

Telling her all too clearly that it was Raphael himself she was attracted to, and not the challenge he represented!

'Where are we going?' Beth prompted in some alarm as she realised they were driving away from London rather than in the direction of her home.

Raphael turned to look at her calmly. 'Your own house proved too difficult to make secure in the time I had available, so we are going to Cesar's estate in Hampshire for a few days until your house has been made ready.'

Beth stared at him. 'Ready for what?'

Raphael's gaze became cool. 'For you to live in, of course.'

'It is ready for me to live in as far as I'm concerned.' She gave a slightly dazed frown. 'What exactly are you doing to the house? And how did you get in? Did Grace give you a key?' she guessed heavily.

'Some days ago.' He nodded curtly. 'Your sister is as concerned for your future welfare as the rest of your family are,' he added as Beth looked hurt at Grace's treachery.

'What exactly are you doing to my house?' she repeated softly.

'Putting in an alarm system. Outside security cameras—Grace does not approve of cameras inside the house,' he explained grimly. 'But there will be alarms on all of the windows, and—'

'Never mind.' Beth waved her hand about weakly in protest at hearing any more of the changes being made to her home without her permission. 'And the estate in Hampshire—are we talking about the same estate where Grace worked for Cesar, and said she felt like a prisoner the whole time she was there?'

'We are, yes.' Raphael gave a slight inclination of his

head. 'But again, if you wish it, the security cameras inside the house can be switched off.'

'But not the sensors on the windows? Or the security codes to get in and out of the doors? Or the dozen or so security guards on the gates and patrolling the grounds?'

His jaw tightened. 'No.'

Beth gave a shake of her head. 'I think you had better turn this car around, after all—'

'Calm yourself, Gabriela—'

'I swear if you call me that name one more time…!'

'Yes?' Raphael arched a cool brow at her vehemence.

'My name is Beth.' She breathed deeply in an effort to remain calm, something that was proving more and more difficult to do around this man. 'I suggest you use it in the future if you want me to answer you.'

He shrugged. 'I did not ask a question but made a statement.'

Beth's gaze narrowed to warning slits. 'Just as I'm stating that I am not staying in some damned prison fortress in the middle of nowhere!'

Raphael held back a smile; if anything, Beth was even more beautiful when she was angry. That beautiful blond hair almost seemed to crackle with electricity. Her eyes glowed. Her creamy cheeks became flushed. The perfect bow of her lips full and slightly parted. And, if he was not mistaken, her nipples were pert and erect beneath the blue sweater she was wearing…

His gaze remained on those aroused breasts as he answered her.

'I trust you will excuse me for correcting you—'

'I don't trust you at all. And I would rather excuse a cobra about to strike than I would you.' Beth continued to glare at him in her frustration.

'Have a care, Beth, or you will turn my head with

all this flattery,' Raphael drawled dryly, eliciting a soft chuckle from the chauffeur beside him.

Beth's eyes glittered darkly. 'I have yet to find anything about you I could be in the least flattering about! Now ask the driver—'

'His name is Edward,' he supplied dryly. 'Edward, meet Miss Navarro.'

'Beth Blake,' she corrected firmly as she smiled at the chauffeur in the driving mirror.

'Miss,' he answered tactfully.

'Would you mind very much turning the car around, Edward, and Raphael will give you the directions to my own home?' She looked challengingly at Raphael even as she spoke to the chauffeur.

Maybe Raphael should have taken his own advice two days ago and put Beth Blake over his knee before spanking her curvaceous backside!

'As I was saying,' he continued coolly, ignoring Beth's instruction and indicating that Edward should do so, too, 'Cesar's estate is not a fortress or a prison, neither is it in the middle of nowhere. There is a town—'

'Ten point two kilometres away, I believe Cesar told Grace when she made a similar comment,' she acknowledged dryly. 'Which, when you're used to living in a city as big and bustling as London, *is* the middle of nowhere. And how am I supposed to get to work every morning? I am not being driven to work in a chauffeur-driven limousine—no offence intended,' she assured Edward distractedly.

'None taken, miss,' he assured her lightly.

'What is wrong with being driven to work in the comfort of a limousine?' Raphael enquired lightly.

Beth gave him an exasperated look. 'I'm a junior assistant in the publicity department.'

'And?'

'And the top executives of the company don't arrive at work in a chauffeur-driven limousine!'

He gave a dismissive shrug of his shoulders. 'That is their loss, of course, but—'

'Raphael, would you try, just for a moment, to put yourself back in the world of us lesser mortals,' she cut in disgustedly, 'instead of this ivory tower Cesar has inhabited for so long and which my sister is trying to drag him from kicking and screaming—and which you appear to have inhabited right alongside him—and realise that in the real world we don't travel in private jets and limousines, but buses and the underground, with maybe the occasional taxi if we're feeling flush.'

He gave a slow considering nod. 'Yes, in those circumstances I can see how this mode of travel might prove a little embarrassing. Understanding your point of view does not mean that I agree with it,' he added wryly as Beth began to smile triumphantly, instantly causing that smile to fade until it was replaced by a frown. 'Cesar gave specific instructions as to your security—'

'And if he told you to go and throw yourself off a bridge would you do that, too?' Beth came back with false sweetness.

Raphael gave a derisive smile. 'Not unless it involved saving you from drowning, no.'

'Then surely there's a little room for manoeuvre on this, too?'

His jaw tightened. 'Manoeuvre, yes, stupidity, no. And it would be the height of stupidity,' he continued firmly as Beth would have spoken, 'for me to allow you to travel about London, or anywhere else, on public transport.'

'You know—' she grimaced '—the sooner you accept that you don't have the right to "allow" me to do anything, then the sooner we're going to be able to come to some sort of arrangement that suits the both of us.'

Raphael gave a confident smile. 'Our present arrangement already suits me perfectly.'

Beth had never felt quite so much as if the unstoppable force had met the immovable object. Or felt so frustrated in regard to her own free will. 'Are you always this stubborn?'

'Is there not a saying "it takes one to know one"?'

She nodded. 'Which doesn't exactly answer my original question, now, does it?'

Raphael appeared to give that question several moments' thought. 'When it comes to security matters, yes, I am always this stubborn,' he finally answered dismissively.

Beth was well aware of her own stubbornness, which didn't mean, as the unstoppable force, that she didn't know when to admit she had been defeated by that immovable object, which in this case happened to be Raphael. 'Fine, I'll go to the estate in Hampshire for a couple of days.' She sighed wearily. 'But I'll need to go back to my house to pick up my work clothes first. After which I will allow myself to be driven to work tomorrow in this limousine. But, whatever ideas you might have to the contrary, I absolutely draw the line on you coming into my workplace with me. Deal?' She looked at him challengingly.

'I am not Cesar—'

'Oh, believe me, I'm well aware of that! Deal?' she prompted again determinedly.

Raphael eyed her steadily for several seconds before nodding tersely. 'Deal.' He turned away to give the driver Beth's home address.

Even so, it felt like a hollow victory to Beth, and one that left her wondering if she had really won anything, or if Raphael hadn't already made contingency plans if she were to make such a request...

* * *

'Grace tells me there's a gym in the east wing of the house?'

Raphael now turned from talking softly to Rodney, the head of Cesar's security in England, having made the introductions when they arrived at the estate in Hampshire a few minutes ago after finding the other man waiting for them in the entrance hall of Cesar's manor house.

Beth had been very quiet since they had driven away from her home earlier, after she had gone upstairs to collect the clothes she had said she needed and left Raphael to talk to the men busy working inside and outside the house. Unusually so, for her.

As he studied her now beneath the light given off by the overhead chandelier Raphael could see that her face was also pale, and her eyes appeared like dark bruises in that pallor. 'Above the guest bedrooms to the right at the top of the staircase, yes…' he confirmed softly.

'Does it have a punch bag in it?'

He raised dark brows. 'With my face painted on it?'

'Preferably, yes. Or Cesar's would do,' she accepted dryly.

Raphael had no idea why it was that this woman made him want to laugh half of the time and strangle her the other half. On this occasion laughter won out, and he chuckled wryly as he turned to dismiss Rodney before answering Beth. 'Not that I am aware of, no, but perhaps a photograph of one of us pinned onto it would do for now?'

'I'm sure it would,' she accepted with a frown.

Raphael frowned as he saw that Beth's eyes, despite her attempts at humour, seemed to be overbright, and not with anger but with tears. 'Are you about to cry?'

Beth almost laughed at the horror she detected in Raphael's tone; like all big strong men, he probably had no idea how to deal with a woman's tears. She almost laughed. Except, she really didn't have anything to laugh about. Cry, yes. Laugh, no. She had believed her situation unbearable while in Argentina, but now they were back in England this nightmare she appeared to be stuck in just kept getting worse.

'Did you even notice the mess those men are making of my home?' She gave a pained wince just at the memory of the army of workmen both inside and outside what had once been her family home, but was now being turned into as much of a secure fortress as this manor house set within its equally secure walls and high gates.

Raphael looked regretful. 'If you had waited a couple of days before going there, as I suggested, it would all have been put back as it was.'

She gave a shake of her head. 'Somehow I doubt that.'

'Beth—'

'Raphael.' She stared up at him steadily.

His mouth thinned. 'I promise you, Beth, your home will be just as you left it by the time we return later in the week.'

'Apart from the fact I can no longer get in my own front door without a security code. Or open the windows without the alarm going off. Or—'

'You are starting to sound like Grace now!'

'Possibly because I now *feel* exactly the same way that Grace does about Cesar's high level of security!' She was breathing hard in her agitation. 'You should be careful, Raphael. If Grace has her way Cesar won't be using that level of security in future, and then you could be out of a job!'

'If so I will simply find another.' He shrugged. 'And I meant that your home will be just as it was in appearance once the work there has been finished. The men working there are experts at what they do.'

'I'm sure they are,' she acknowledged flatly. 'If you'll excuse me, I really think I need to go upstairs and find the gym—before I decide not to wait and just punch you on the jaw right now for want of a better target!'

He raised dark brows. 'I thought I was the target?'

She breathed in deeply. 'No, at the moment that's Cesar.' She breathed out just as deeply. 'And I need to work off some of this excess energy before I really do hit something. Or someone!' she added grimly.

'It is almost time for dinner...'

'So it is.' She smiled slightly. 'And it's just dawned on me that Cesar's cook is currently in Argentina with him making arrangements for their wedding next month. And if you're expecting me to cook dinner for you instead then you're going to be out of luck. Grace is the cook in our family,' she added with satisfaction as Raphael looked decidedly crestfallen by her announcement.

'You can't cook?'

'Of course I can cook, I just don't intend to do so,' Beth corrected, starting to relax and once again enjoy herself. 'How about you, Raphael? Can you cook?'

'Steak and baked potato when I have to...'

'Then this would appear to be one of the occasions when you have to.' Beth nodded her satisfaction. 'At least, until Kevin Maddox can organise Grace's replacement.' She had yet to meet Cesar's English PA, but Grace had seemed to like him the previous month when he interviewed her for the job as Cesar's cook/housekeeper.

'And you will deign to make the salad?'

Her eyes glowed with humour. 'Oh, I think I might agree to do that, yes.'

He gave a terse inclination of his head. 'Then we will make dinner together later.'

Beth wasn't sure that 'togetherness' with this particular

man was something she wanted. Or was in the least wise, when she seemed to be becoming more and more physically aware of Raphael the more time they spent together...

She nodded. 'In the meantime, I'll go upstairs and choose my own bedroom from the rooms in the east wing, shall I?' She turned and took the first step up the huge curved staircase before pausing to look back at Raphael over her shoulder. 'If you would just arrange for my luggage to be delivered up to my room so that I can change before I go in search of the gym...'

Raphael's jaw looked tense. 'You were wrong two days ago, Beth.'

She raised her brows. 'Wrong about what?'

'You appear to be learning all too quickly how to behave as that "pampered poodle" you spoke of so disparagingly!' He eyed her scathingly.

Beth's breath caught in her throat, knowing that Raphael had meant to wound with his remark. And that he had succeeded. She didn't want any part of being Gabriela Navarro. Not the name. Or to be thought of as that spoilt and pampered little-rich-girl Raphael had just referred to so scathingly.

Beth had sincerely hoped that once she returned to England she would be able to get some perspective back into her life—albeit with Raphael lurking somewhere in the background—but instead she hadn't even been allowed to return to her own home, let alone the normality of her life.

She drew in a shaky breath before speaking. 'That was very unkind of you.'

His mouth twisted. 'I was not aware that you required kindness from me?'

'Everyone prefers kindness to cruelty, Raphael.'

He breathed deeply. 'Perhaps I am not feeling particularly kind.'

Beth frowned. 'Because I asked for my bags to be brought upstairs?'

No, Raphael's present mood had very little to do with Beth's perfectly valid request, and more to do with the fact that he had just become aware of the fact that the two of them would be staying in this house alone for the next few days. Something that hadn't occurred to him until just now.

Beth's slightly bewildered expression at his unexpected aggression certainly wasn't helping him to remain professionally aloof from this situation. Possibly because 'professional' was the last thing he felt whenever he was in this woman's company. And, if Raphael was to do his job of protecting her properly, he needed to remain completely detached as well as professional.

He looked at her coolly. 'I will arrange for your bags to be brought upstairs.'

Beth looked at him searchingly for several long seconds before nodding slowly, her eyes looking even darker in the pallor of her face. 'Thank you.'

He raised dark brows. 'No comment as to the fact that should have been my original answer?'

'No.'

Raphael allowed himself a small smile. 'Are you feeling quite well?'

A pained looked crossed Beth's expressive face. 'Not really. Will you excuse me?' She turned sharply before running quickly up the stairs.

Raphael remained in the hallway, hands clenched at his sides as he continued to watch her as she reached the top of those stairs, before turning to the right and disappearing down the hallway in the direction of the guest bedrooms in the east wing. As if the devil himself were following at her heels...

Should Raphael follow her, and apologise—once

again!—for appearing insensitive to her obvious distress, both at thoughts of being Gabriela Navarro and the sudden changes that were being asked—no, demanded!—of her because of it? Or would his apology only succeed in making this situation worse?

Raphael wasn't sure their present situation—alone together and at constant loggerheads—could get any worse!

And yet he had made a promise to Cesar before leaving Buenos Aires, and to Esther and Carlos, who were both so obviously distraught at the thought of their daughter leaving them again so soon after they had found her.

A promise that he would protect Beth at all costs.

Raphael just hadn't realised, when he had made that promise, that he might be asked to protect Beth from himself.

CHAPTER FOUR

'BETH?' RAPHAEL CAME to a halt in the open bedroom door-way as he saw—and heard—her crying as she lay face down on the bed, immediately dropping the two bags he was carrying to cross the bedroom in long determined strides before sitting down on the bed beside her.

The first Beth knew of Raphael's presence in the bed-room with her was when she felt the bed dipping beside her before his hands came to rest gently on her shoulders as he turned her over. His arms moved about her as he took one look at her tear-stained face before pulling her towards him and cradling her against the reassuring heat of his chest.

That gentleness, along with Raphael's reassuring warmth, and the steady beat of his heart beneath her cheek, only made Beth cry all the harder.

These past few days had been—Beth couldn't even begin to describe how awful they had been!

Going back to Buenos Aires with Grace. Seeing her own likeness to the Navarros, most especially to Esther. Even the similarity of her own stubborn determination to Cesar's impossible arrogance! And the results of those blood tests, no matter how much Beth verbally denied it, had completely unsettled her.

To the point that she had desperately needed to escape,

to flee the demand being made of her to accept she was Gabriela Navarro and not Beth Blake.

But returning to England, seeing the alterations being made on her home, arriving at Cesar's estate, with its high walls and dozen or so security guards, had only succeeded in making the possibility of her really being Gabriela Navarro seem all the more real, not less so.

More real than Beth could emotionally deal with.

It was too much. All of it. The whole idea, of her being—becoming, the Argentinian heiress Gabriela Navarro was so totally off the charts of Beth's comprehension that, no matter how she might try to pretend and behave to the contrary, Beth knew she was in serious danger of being totally overwhelmed by it all.

Even the name Gabriela was foreign to her.

Gabriela Esther Carlotta Navarro. Esther for her mother, Carlotta in memory of Carlos Navarro's mother...

And how could that possibly be Beth, when she barely understood a word of Spanish, let alone spoke it?

It couldn't be.

And yet somewhere, deep inside her, Beth had the uneasy—the unacceptable!—feeling that it really was...

She moistened her lips with the tip of her tongue. 'Do you believe that I'm her, too?'

'Yes.'

Raphael was so much like Cesar: no ifs, ands or buts, just that harsh and implacable affirmative! 'What makes you so certain?' Beth frowned up at him.

He breathed deeply. 'You could not possibly remember me, but—I knew Cesar's sister as a baby.'

Her eyes widened. 'I didn't realise that...'

He smiled tightly 'There is no reason why you should have done so. But yes, I am as convinced as everyone else that you are Gabriela Navarro.'

'Why?'

'Obviously you look so much like Esther and Carlos. And you are as fiercely stubborn as Cesar when you argue,' he added teasingly. 'But I can also see traces of that much younger Gabriela in you, too. She was utterly adorable and charming, even at two years of age, but also very determined in her nature, decided what she wanted or where she needed to be, and ensured that she got there.' He chuckled softly.

Beth eyed him teasingly. 'You think I'm adorable and charming?'

'And, do not forget, very determined,' he reminded her lightly.

'But what if I still don't *want* to be her?' Beth demanded distractedly, still trying to assimilate the information that she—Gabriela—and Raphael had known each other over twenty years ago. And that Raphael had obviously felt the same brotherly indulgent affection for Gabriela as Cesar had.

'Is that the reason you are upset?'

'Yes,' she admitted huskily.

'Then I would say that you are unique in not wishing to be the young, beautiful, and very wealthy Navarro heiress,' Raphael drawled dryly.

Beth sighed heavily. 'Everyone dreams of being wealthy enough to one day not have to worry about money again. But not at the sacrifice of their other hopes and dreams.'

'And what are your other hopes and dreams?'

'To become the best editor I know how to be, and maybe even find and edit that one special book that's going to take the world by storm!' she revealed fiercely.

'And you do not believe you can do those things as Gabriela Navarro?'

'I know I can't!'

'The Gabriela I knew all those years ago would have ensured that she did exactly as she wished to do in her adult life,' Raphael said softly.

'Cesar's answer to that would seem to be to simply buy a publishing company for me,' she muttered disgustedly.

He smiled ruefully. 'That is the way Cesar deals with such problems. It does not have to be your way also.'

'No,' Beth acknowledged doubtfully.

'Take a deep breath and learn to deal with one problem at a time, Beth,' Raphael advised huskily. 'If you stop and consider, you have already done so. You are here, back in England, as you wished to be, and tomorrow you will return to your job, also as you wished,' he explained as she looked up at him questioningly. 'You have free will, Beth, are over twenty-one, and so at liberty to live your life in any way that you choose.'

'And you think that the Navarros and Cesar are going to accept that?' She smiled ruefully.

'I think the Gabriela I knew would have made sure they were given no choice in the matter!' he assured her dryly.

Beth exhaled shakily as she realised she had been holding her breath for several minutes. And Raphael was right, of course; no matter what the family pressure—whichever family that might happen to be!—she ultimately didn't have to do anything she didn't want to do.

And at the moment what she wanted to do was try to repair the damage she had done to the soggy mess that was now Raphael's white silk shirt! 'I'm so sorry about this.' She attempted to brush away some of that dampness with her hand.

'Why is it that women never have a handkerchief or a tissue with them when they cry?' Raphael's voice was a teasing rumble beneath her cheek. 'Here, use this,' he encouraged softly as she made no effort to take the blue silk handkerchief that she knew had been in his breast pocket until a few seconds ago, as a match for the neatly knotted tie at his throat and the colour of his eyes.

'We don't decide to cry, it just happens.' Beth took the handkerchief from him and mopped at the dampness of his shirt before drying her cheeks and blowing her nose. 'And how many women have you made cry?' she murmured as she tucked the silk handkerchief into her denims pocket, intending to wash it before returning it to him.

'None that I recall.'

She gave him a derisive glance. 'Why do I find that so hard to believe?'

He raised dark brows. 'I do not know. Why do you?'

Now there was a trick question if ever Beth had heard one!

How did she know women had cried over this man? This man who was as handsome as sin, and just as wickedly dangerous? And unattainable...

Beneath those breathtaking good looks and unmistakeable sensuality, Beth sensed there was an aloofness to Raphael Cordoba, a coldness that said his heart had never been touched by any of the women he might have been involved with since he reached sexual maturity. An aloofness, and coldness of emotions, that challenged at the same time as it gave warning of heartbreak to any who ventured forth.

So, yes, whether Raphael had witnessed it or not, Beth was certain that there had been many women who had cried tears over him. 'Just a hunch.' She shrugged dismissively. 'You so obviously spoke from experience about ladies not having a handkerchief with them when they cry.'

'I have six sisters, so yes—'

'Six sisters!' Beth pulled back slightly to look up at

him in disbelief, disconcerted by the admission. 'Older or younger, or a mixture of the two?'

'All older.' He grimaced.

She gave a slightly dazed shake of her head. 'I can't even begin to think what it must have been like growing up with six older sisters…'

'The fights that ensued over the use of the bathrooms were always entertaining,' he revealed dryly.

'I would imagine so…'

He shrugged. 'But being a young boy, with the usual aversion to bathing, helped in that situation, I believe.'

Beth tried to imagine Raphael as a young boy. No doubt his hair would have been longer then, more inclined to curl, and those piercing blue eyes wouldn't have that hard cynicism to them that had come with maturity—

Or perhaps they would?

She knew nothing of Raphael's background but the things he had chosen to reveal to her over the past few days—and she hadn't felt inclined to ask Grace anything about him, either, knowing exactly what conclusions her sister would have drawn from Beth's interest in the personal life of Cesar's enigmatic Head of Security!

But Raphael had just revealed that he was the youngest of seven children, which surely meant that his family home would have to have been cramped and overcrowded, and that so many children would have been a severe strain on the family finances. A hardship that would only have been made more painfully obvious by Raphael's friendship with a man whose family was as rich and powerful as Cesar Navarro's. A friendship that had perhaps come into existence because Raphael's family lived and worked on one of the Navarro properties?

'Are all of your sisters married?'

'Five of them. Rosa is…slower, than others,' Raphael

revealed tightly. 'It is not hereditary, you understand—it was caused by complications at her birth.'

'I wasn't presuming that it was,' Beth answered him distractedly, thinking of the fact that Raphael's parents would have had five weddings to pay for, if not dowries to supply—did the parents still provide dowries for their daughters in Argentina?—as well as the continuing financial support of their remaining daughter. Perhaps Raphael even helped with that support; he had certainly sounded defensive just now on his sister Rosa's behalf. 'Does Rosa still live at home with your parents?'

His eyes hardened. 'She resides with my eldest sister, Delores, and her family.'

'But none of your family live in Buenos Aires?' she prompted curiously.

'No.' Raphael now sounded, and looked, just as unapproachable on the subject of his family as he had two days ago.

'And what of your parents? Are they both still alive?'

'My father is. My mother died shortly after my tenth birthday.'

Beth gave a pained frown. 'I'm sorry.'

He shrugged. 'So am I.'

'It can't have been easy for your father to bring up all those children on his own.'

'He remarried when I was sixteen.' Raphael's jaw had become inflexible.

As evidence that he didn't like his stepmother? Perhaps this was the reason Rosa lived with her eldest sister, and perhaps another reason why Beth always sensed a stiltedness in Raphael's manner whenever his family was mentioned in conversation.

She had sensed some sort of tension between Raphael and his family when Esther had enquired after them two days ago. Possibly one that had been created by Raphael's desire to escape from his father's second marriage as well as the poverty of his childhood...

That need to escape would certainly fit in with the years he had spent in the military. It would also explain the impatience he showed towards Beth's rejection of the idea of becoming a member of the wealthy Navarro family.

Raphael had absolutely no idea what thoughts were going through Beth's head at that moment, but whatever they were they had brought a frown to her creamy brow. Just as he was aware of the frown between his own eyes as he realised he was sitting on the side of the bed with Beth cradled in his arms...

Despite her outer veneer of toughness, Beth felt utterly soft and very feminine with her breasts pressing against the hardness of his chest, her back feeling softly sensual as his hands ran lightly over the material of her T-shirt, the softness of her silky blond hair smelling of citrus fruits, her perfume—something lightly floral and utterly feminine that was uniquely Beth—having invaded his senses and at the same time lowered his defences.

Defences Raphael knew he could not allow to be lowered with a woman he found as beautiful and intriguingly enticing as he did Beth Blake. Even less so in regard to Gabriela Navarro, the woman he was here to protect.

He removed his arms abruptly before standing up and moving sharply away from her. 'If you like I will take you upstairs now and show you the gym?'

She blinked at the sudden change of subject, before that surprise was quickly masked and she smiled brightly. 'Feel like joining me?'

Raphael's lids narrowed warily. 'Sorry?'

She stood up, lean and slender in a blue sweater and

fitted low-rider denims. 'Grace said that you and Cesar often spar together in the gym...'

'Yes.'

She grinned. 'I have a black belt in karate.'

Raphael drew in a sharp breath. 'And you are suggesting that the two of us should now spar together,' he murmured doubtfully.

She quirked a mocking brow. 'Is your reluctance because I'm a woman?'

'My reluctance has nothing to do with your being a woman—' He broke off as she gave a disparaging snort. 'It has nothing to do with your being a woman, Beth,' he insisted firmly, 'and everything to do with the fact that I was in a special unit of the Argentinian army for several years.'

'And?' She shrugged.

'And I have...skills that are far beyond those of karate,' he explained grimly.

'And would those skills include knowing how to disarm and kill someone with your bare hands?'

'If necessary, yes,' he admitted harshly.

None of Beth's inner shock showed in her expression— why should it, when she had already guessed, from the predatory stillness that always surrounded Raphael, that he could be lethal, physically as well as emotionally? 'And have you ever felt it necessary?'

'Yes.' A nerve pulsed in the tension of his jaw.

'Well, let's hope you won't find it necessary today,' she dismissed lightly.

'Beth—'

'Oh, come on, Raphael, hand-to-hand combat is going to be much more fun than that punch bag with your own or Cesar's photo pinned on it!'

He drew in a deep, controlling breath. 'Not if you are the one who ends up black and blue.'

'And is that likely to happen?'

'Not if I can avoid it, no,' he bit out grimly.

Beth looked at him searchingly for several seconds, once again noting that quiet but lethal strength that proclaimed him a predator; the clenched fists at his sides, the determined set of his jaw and the piercing blue of his narrowed eyes. All indications that this man, beneath the expensive trappings of civility he wore so well—those designer label suits, and the silk shirts and ties—was in fact a fighting machine. Lean, dangerous and, by his own admission, ultimately deadly.

And yet…

'I trust you not to hurt me, Raphael,' she assured him huskily.

He blinked. 'You trust me?'

'Not to physically hurt me, yes.' Emotionally was another matter, however…

Beth's emotions in regard to the Navarro family might have knocked her emotions all over the place at the moment, but not so much that she didn't know how physically attracted she was to Raphael—or how much of a mistake it would be for her to allow it to become anything more than that. That dark edge of danger, clinging to him like a second skin, was also a warning to any and all who might try to get to the emotions hidden beneath that skin.

The broodingly dangerous Raphael Cordoba was way, way out of her league.

Those piercing blue eyes glowed fiercely for several seconds. 'Very well.' He nodded abruptly. 'I will leave you to change while I go and do the same, and meet you upstairs in the gym on the floor above this one in ten minutes.' He turned on his heel and strode from the bedroom as suddenly as he had entered it.

Leaving Beth to stare after him as she wondered how

many times Raphael had been called upon to use those specialised skills, both during his years in the army and the past ten years he had spent as Cesar's Head of Security.

Out of her league or not, Beth would have to be made of steel not to be affected by Raphael's appearance when she met him upstairs in the gym ten minutes later!

A black sleeveless vest clung to the perfectly muscled contours of his chest, revealing equally muscular and smoothly bronzed arms, the silky dark hair on his chest visible above the low neckline of that sleeveless vest, loose-fitting soft black cotton trousers resting low down on the leanness of his hips, his legs long and powerful, his feet bare. He looked every bit a bronzed sculpture, the swarthiness of his face harshly chiselled, every part of that lean and muscled body perfectly toned.

'Ready?'

Beth had to drag her gaze up from all that muscled perfection in order to meet his piercing blue gaze. Her throat moved as she swallowed before attempting to answer him off-handedly. 'Don't I look ready?'

Oh, yes, she looked ready—but for what, Raphael was unsure. Her blond hair was secured back in a tight plait down the length of her spine, and she was wearing a vest top and loose trousers similar to his own. Perfectly suitable attire in which to fight. An impression that was totally nullified by the full swell of her breasts beneath that white vest-top, the nipples pressing against that light material revealed as being dark and dusky—and just as plump and aroused as the berries they resembled.

And she was expecting Raphael to fight her when she looked like that?

'Cesar never does anything by halves, does he?' Beth looked about her appreciatively at all of the state-of-the-art equipment: several sets of weights, a running machine, rowing machine, several other bits of equipment that she had no idea what they were used for, along with a sauna and a shower, and a blue martial arts mat that dominated the centre of the room.

'Not even falling in love,' Raphael acknowledged dryly.

Beth turned to smile at him as she slipped off her flip-flops beside the mat. 'And he does love my big sister, Grace, very much, doesn't he?'

He nodded. 'She is more than woman enough to match Cesar's strength of character, yes.'

Beth's smile faded as she felt a sharp pang of—of what, at Raphael's obvious admiration for Grace? Jealousy? Towards her own sister? Surely not? Although there was no doubting Raphael's admiration for Grace. 'Do I detect a slight infatuation for my big sister, Raphael?' she taunted in an effort to cover up her discomfort at the mere idea of Raphael being interested in Grace.

He raised dark brows. 'Infatuation is for adolescents.'

His slightly contemptuous tone implied he obviously considered her amongst that category—not a cheering thought when Beth only had to look at him to feel that tug of desire in the pit of her stomach.

'Maybe a little lust, then?' she came back tartly.

His mouth thinned disapprovingly. 'That would be entirely inappropriate in regard to the future wife of the man to whom I am as close as a brother.'

Beth shot him a scathing glance. 'That wouldn't necessarily stop you from feeling that way inside.'

'I do not feel lustful towards your sister!' A nerve pulsed in Raphael's tightly clenched jaw.

'Protest much?' she came back tautly.

Raphael regarded her through narrowed lids, easily noting the glitter—of scorn or anger, he was not sure—in the dark brown depths of her eyes, the slight curl to her top lip, her chin tilted up in challenge. 'Are you attempting to bait me, Beth?' he finally murmured softly.

She shrugged bared shoulders. 'Merely trying to ascertain how you feel towards my big sister, and whether or not someone should warn Cesar he has a rival.'

'You?'

'No, not me.' She sighed her impatience. 'Cesar is altogether too arrogant as it is. A little healthy competition would do his overinflated ego the world of good!'

'Grace has earned my admiration and respect, nothing more,'

Raphael bit out tautly.

'Lucky Grace…'

He eyed Beth sharply as he heard her softly murmured response. Because she did not believe she had also earned his admiration and respect? Did Beth *want* his admiration and respect? Somehow he very much doubted that; Beth Blake gave the impression that she didn't want or require any man's admiration and respect!

'Shall we?' she prompted sharply as she stepped onto the mat.

Raphael's mouth twisted derisively as he took in Beth's fighting stance at the same time as his gaze lingered on the utter femininity of the red painted nails on her bared feet.

'Don't let them fool you,' Beth assured him tauntingly as she saw the direction of Raphael's slightly contemptuous blue gaze. 'And don't hold back, either,' she warned as he stepped onto the mat and faced her.

A warning she soon had reason to regret when, despite that black belt in karate, she found herself thrown flat on her back three times in as many minutes, and knocking all of the air out of her lungs each time it happened!

She stood up after the last throw, breathing hard, but

more determined than ever as she saw that Raphael hadn't even broken out in a sweat from their exertions, whereas the last few minutes had not only freed several untidy tendrils of her hair from its confining plait, but also reduced her to being, not only sticky hot, but decidedly out of breath. 'Is that the best you have?' she taunted.

Raphael gave a grimly wicked smile. 'I am just warming up.'

That was what Beth was afraid of!

'You have tells, you know,' he added with infuriating calm.

She blinked. 'What?'

He shrugged those deliciously muscled and bronzed shoulders. 'You glance very slightly to whichever side you intend to throw me, allowing me to shift balance in preparation for that attack.'

'I do not!'

'Oh, yes.' Raphael nodded. 'In the same way that a poker player might remain still when he has a good hand of cards, but cannot stop himself from pulling on his ear lobe when he is about to make a bluff call.'

She would show him 'tells'…!

'Now you are concentrating too hard on not revealing those tells rather than the moves you are about to make,' Raphael drawled a few seconds later as Beth once again lay flat on her back at his bared feet.

'Has anyone ever told you that you're incredibly annoying?' Beth muttered as she sat up.

'It has been mentioned before, yes.' He grinned unabashedly. 'And implied several times by you, too, I believe.'

She later blamed that grin for what happened next—that self-satisfied and wholly superior grin!—because it wasn't just annoying, it was infuriating!

So much so that Beth reacted purely on instinct, her feet lashing out at Raphael's calves, his grin completely disappearing as she followed that kick with a scissor movement that totally knocked him off his feet, allowing Beth to leap on top of him, her body lying flush with his as she pinned his shoulders to the mat.

Only to then become totally aware of every lean and muscled inch of him. Including the hard and pulsing length of his arousal pressing into the soft well between her thighs…!

CHAPTER FIVE

'WHAT HAPPENS NOW?' Raphael prompted huskily, his breath a soft caress against Beth's heated cheeks as he looked up at her between narrowed lids, making no attempt to move out from beneath her much softer curves.

Her throat moved convulsively as she swallowed, her cheeks flushed, that gleam of triumph slowly fading from her eyes to be replaced by wariness as she obviously became fully aware of the precariousness of her position.

The pink tip of her tongue appeared between her lips as she moistened them before answering him softly. 'I'm not really sure...'

Neither was Raphael. Instinct—and the demands of his aroused body—told him to wrap his arms about this woman before rolling over and putting her beneath him, to nudge her legs apart before settling between them as he kissed her into pleasurable submission. Logic and good sense told him that would not only be an incredibly stupid move on his part, but also a dangerous one.

As he had feared, his instinct won...

'What—?' Beth barely had time to voice a protest as she felt steel bands move about her waist—Raphael's arms?—as he rolled to the side and then above her, pinning her hands with his either side of her head, before his lips—those sculptured and incredibly sensual lips!—came down and claimed hers in a kiss that sent any thought of further protest completely out of her head. A kiss that owed nothing to gentle exploration and everything to fierce, possessive need as Raphael's lips devoured and claimed.

Beth returned that hunger, her lips parting as Raphael's tongue moved across them in a rasping caress before plunging deeply, hotly, into the heat of her mouth. She arched beneath him as he moved his thighs against and into her in a slow and seductive rhythm, freeing her hands to move them caressingly over the muscled contours of his chest to the warmth of his naked shoulders and then down over the flexing muscles of his back to the firmness of his bottom.

Steel encased in velvet. Every hard, delicious inch of Raphael was solid muscle encased in velvet-soft flesh. His chest. Shoulders. Back. Bottom. The hard and throbbing length of his aroused shaft as it moved so enticingly between her thighs…!

This man, a man Beth had once accused of possessing the emotions of a robot, was as physically aroused as she was!

She groaned low in her throat as she felt one of Raphael's hands now cupping her breast, the thin material of her T-shirt no barrier to the pleasure of the sweeping caress of his thumb across the achingly aroused nipple, and sending shards of that pleasure coursing through her body even as it increased the throbbing, damp heat between her swollen and moist thighs.

Beth gazed up at Raphael in mute appeal as he wrenched his mouth from hers to move his weight off her as he looked down at her searchingly with eyes that were as dark as midnight, a flush to the hardness of his cheeks.

'Your breasts fit perfectly into the palm of my hand,' he murmured gruffly.

'Do they?' The sexual tension between them was so heavy and thick with expectation that Beth could barely breathe.

'I wonder if...' Those sculptured lips slightly parted as he continued to hold her gaze as he slowly lowered his head and placed his mouth on her breasts through her T-shirt before he gently drew the tight bud of her nipple into the heat of his mouth and suckled deeply.

Beth's lids fluttered closed, her breath now coming in ragged gasps as she instinctively arched her back, pushing her nipple deeper into the burning heat of Raphael's mouth, wanting more, wanting— Oh, God, wanting—

She gasped, her fingers digging painfully into Raphael's shoulders, as she felt the heat of his hand cup between her parted thighs before pressing against the swollen nub nestled there in the same rhythm as he suckled deeply on her aching nipple, Beth immediately becoming lost to this duel assault on her senses, the pleasure rising, and then rising higher still, until she felt on the point of—

A deep gurgling sound preceded a low rumble, breaking through that haze of pleasure as Raphael stilled above her before releasing her nipple and raising his head to look down at her enquiringly, his eyes glittering a dark and amused blue.

Beth licked her lips. 'Was that my stomach rumbling or yours?'

His mouth quirked into a mocking smile. 'I believe it was yours...'

How embarrassing was that? She was alone with, and being kissed by, the most gorgeously handsome man she had ever met in her life, the two of them were making love together—to the degree she was poised on the edge of climax!—and her uncooperative stomach chose that moment to let her know it was time she put some food inside it!

Something that Raphael, at least, found amusing, if the laughter gleaming in those dark blue eyes as he looked down at her was any indication.

'It is past time you were fed, it would seem,' he bit out harshly. He rose agilely to his feet before holding out his hand to help Beth stand up beside him, the expression in his eyes hidden by hooded lids.

A Beth who was totally aware of the dampness of her T-shirt against her bared breast, as indication of the intimacies they had just shared...

Intimacies Raphael gave no indication of so much as remembering, let alone being affected by, fifteen minutes later as he moved efficiently about the kitchen preparing the steaks and potatoes for their dinner, while Beth washed and prepared the salad.

Beth didn't know whether to be relieved or irritated by his behaviour. A lot of both, perhaps. Relieved that she wasn't being put through feeling awkward in his company. But irritated, just the same, by the way Raphael seemed to have succeeded in putting the incident—apocalyptic as far as Beth was concerned!—completely from his mind. She had dated often in the past, even shared a passionate kiss or two with several of the men she had dated, but she had never been aroused by those kisses in the way she was even now just being in the same room with Raphael, let alone allowed them to touch her intimately. More than touch her intimately...!

Her gaze had avoided meeting Raphael's earlier as she had mumbled her excuses before stumbling from the gym and hurrying down to her bedroom, breathing a sigh of relief once she was able to lean back against the closed bedroom door. Which was when she had caught sight of her reflection in the dressing-table mirror directly across from her...

Her hair was a tangled mess as it escaped the confines of her plait, her eyes looked feverishly bright, her cheeks flushed, lips slightly swollen, but worst of all had been the sight of the damp patch on the left side of her T-shirt, that moisture making the white material almost transparent, and so blatantly revealing the turgid ripeness of her nipple...!

A nipple still red and achingly engorged from the intimate ministrations of Raphael's lips, tongue and teeth, Beth had discovered when she drew the T-shirt over her head before throwing it across the room in disgust.

Which was why, once she had showered, she had chosen to dress in a black bra beneath a black blouse over the top of faded denims, before brushing her hair dry so that it lay in a soft and silky sheen against the black blouse.

A pale foundation had taken care of her flushed cheeks, but there was very little Beth could do to hide the fact that her lips remained slightly puffy and swollen from the fierceness of the kisses she and Raphael had shared...

Not that she need have worried too much about her appearance when Raphael—again looking dangerously handsome in a black T-shirt and black denims—had only given her a cursory glance as she entered the kitchen, before then proceeding to continue preparing dinner as if she weren't there.

Which only succeeded in increasing her feelings of irritation. 'Would you prefer to eat in here or in the dining room?' she prompted sharply.

'In here is fine.' Raphael didn't so much as glance her way as he grilled the steaks.

'Scared I might misunderstand if we were to eat in the formal dining room together, with maybe a candle or two alight in the middle of the table?' Beth taunted as she placed knives and forks on the kitchen table for the two of them, along with the condiments.

Raphael did glance back at her then. 'Very little scares me, Beth,' he assured her coolly.

A coolness that only made Beth's temper burn even hotter. 'So we're just going to pretend earlier didn't happen?'

He raised dark brows. 'I had hoped so, but obviously I was wrong.'

Her hands clenched at her sides. 'Don't take that superior tone with me.'

'What tone do you want me to take, Beth?' Raphael sighed as he turned fully to face her. 'Or perhaps you require an apology?' He grimaced. 'Very well. I should not have kissed you earlier, let alone touched you in the way that I did—'

'You're just making the situation worse!'

Raphael didn't see how it could get any worse. He had overstepped a line earlier, had breeched that barrier so necessary between protector and the person being protected. A lapse in judgement that seriously jeopardised his ability to protect Beth in the way that she should be protected. A breach, if Beth's challenging behaviour now was an indication, she was unwilling to overlook, and so making it impossible for Raphael to do so, either.

He frowned grimly. 'I believe it would be better, for both of us, if we were to forgot what happened earlier—'

'Can you forget it?'

His jaw clenched. 'Yes.'

'Well, isn't that just convenient?' Her eyes flashed darkly. 'Unfortunately I don't have your selective memory.'

Raphael ground his back teeth together before speaking. 'There is absolutely nothing wrong with my memory, Beth.'

'Then—'

'Do you not understand I have a job to do?' Raphael rasped harshly as he gave up all pretence of politeness in the face of Beth's dogged determination to have this conversation—whether he wished it or not. 'And I cannot do that job properly, cannot protect you in the way that you need to be protected, if my thoughts are distracted by images of making love with you! There—does that answer your question?' He glared his displeasure as a nerve pulsed in his tightly clenched jaw.

'As a matter of fact, it does.' She relaxed back against the table edge as she looked across the kitchen at him challengingly. 'It distracts you to think of the two of us making love together?'

Raphael drew in a harsh breath. 'Yes!'

'It distracts me, too,' she admitted huskily.

His eyes narrowed. 'You—'

'Raphael—'

'You will do me the courtesy of allowing me to finish,' he rasped impatiently.

'But—'

'Beth!' He bit out his frustration.

'Fine.' Beth held up her hands in defeat. 'I was only going to tell you that the steaks are on fire, but if you aren't inter—' She broke off with a grin as Raphael turned and began swearing as he saw the flames and smoke coming out of the grill pan. 'Don't worry,' she added lightly as he pulled the pan out onto the trivet before beating the flames out with the tea towel. 'I've always preferred my steaks well done, anyway!'

Raphael shot her a venomous glance. 'I have not.'

'Poor you,' she murmured dryly.

'Can we just get this meal over and done with?' Raphael all but threw the two steaks onto the waiting plates. 'I have work to do this evening.'

Beth pulled out a chair and sat down. 'Anything I can help you with?' If she were at home then she could have spent the evening with friends, or catching up on house-work, maybe even watching one of her favourite DVDs, but she had no idea what she was supposed to do with the rest of her evening stuck out here in the wilds of Hampshire.

'I think you have "helped" me quite enough for one eve-ning!' Raphael pulled out the chair opposite before folding his long length down onto it.

'If you're sure…' Beth helped herself to salad before pushing the bowl across the table to him.

'I am very sure.'

She nodded as she cut off a piece of steak before pop-ping it into her mouth and chewing with obvious enjoy-ment for several seconds. 'Mmm, this steak is delicious.'

Raphael wasn't fooled for a moment by the innocence of Beth's expression as she looked across the table at him, knew, by the laughter gleaming in the darkness of her eyes and the half-smile on those thoroughly kissed lips, that her earlier bad humour had now evaporated and she was en-joying herself. At his expense.

'My father would weep if he could see how I have mas-sacred his precious beef,' he muttered disgustedly as he pushed the burnt offering to the side of his plate.

'Your father's beef?'

Raphael nodded. 'Cesar has it flown here from Ar-gentina.'

'Your father farms cattle?' she prompted lightly.

Raphael gave her a derisive glance. 'Cattle are not farmed in Argentina, they are ranched. By gauchos.'

Beth had seen photos in magazines of gauchos; men as

hard and rugged as the terrain they worked on. 'And your father works on a ranch in Argentina?'

His jaw tightened as he seemed to realise he had once again been drawn into talking about his family. 'On the pampas, yes.'

'That's very rough countryside, isn't it?'

'Very,' Raphael acknowledged tersely, that stern set to his jaw telling Beth that he would not be drawn on the subject any further than that.

'Does—? Oh, damn, I forgot the wine!' She gave him an apologetic grimace as she stood up, having opened a bottle of red wine when she first came down to the kitchen in order to let it breathe, as Grace had shown her. 'Here, maybe it will help your steak go down!' She sat down to pour wine into one of the two empty glasses on the table before filling her own and then placing the bottle in the middle of the table.

'I doubt anything would succeed in making this shoe leather palatable!' Raphael muttered disgustedly as he lifted the glass to his lips and took a sip of the wine.

There was absolutely no way of missing the way that he stilled the moment he tasted the wine before slowly swallowing. 'Is there something wrong with it?' Beth prompted warily as she paused after sipping her own wine; Grace might have shown her how to remove the cork from a bottle of wine, and how to chill a white wine, and allow a bottle of red to breathe before drinking it, but differentiating between a good and a cheap and nasty wine was still beyond Beth's palate.

Raphael carefully replaced his glass down on the table. 'Where did you get this from?'

'The rack near the kitchen door. Which was why I assumed it was okay to use. Please tell me I haven't opened some priceless and irreplaceable bottle of wine that Cesar has been nurturing as an investment, or saving for a special occasion!' She wasn't feeling in the least reassured by the bleakness of Raphael's expression.

Raphael affected a neutral expression as he reached out to pick up the bottle and look at the label. As he had thought, it bore the Cordoba name. His name. From his family vineyard.

'Raphael?'

He forced the tension from his shoulders as he glanced across the table at the anxiously watching Beth. 'No, you have not opened a priceless bottle of wine,' he drawled reassuringly as he replaced the bottle carefully back onto the table. 'I had forgotten that Cesar is partial to this particular red wine with his steak, that is all.' He gave a shake of his head.

Beth reached out and picked up the bottle, a frown appearing between her eyes as she read the name on the label. 'A relative of yours?'

Raphael gave a humourless smile. 'My father.'

She sat back against the chair. 'But I thought you said your father was a gaucho?'

'I said he ranched cattle,' Raphael corrected dryly.

'But I thought— He *owns* the ranch,' Beth realised with a frown, 'and no doubt has gauchos who work for him? Just as he owns the vineyard where this wine came from?'

He gave a grimace. 'Yes.'

'Your family is wealthy?'

His mouth twisted derisively. 'Nowhere near the Navarros' fortune, but, yes, the Cordoba family is wealthy.'

'I had assumed—' She blinked. 'Assumption obviously being the mother of all—'

'Beth!' he cut in warningly.

She gave him an impatient glare. 'Well, you have to admit, Raphael, it's a little unusual, to find the heir to a ranch and an obviously successful vineyard working as Head of Security for someone else, even if that someone else is as close to you as a brother.'

A nerve pulsed in Raphael's tightly clenched jaw. 'Not if that is what that person chooses to do.'

'But you're the son and heir, so why aren't you working on the ranch or vineyard with your father?'

'I do not believe I have to answer that.'

'Why not, when it's a perfectly valid question in the circumstances?'

Beth could have no idea of the circumstances surrounding Raphael's reasons for leaving his home and his family fifteen years ago, and moving to Buenos Aires to stay with the Navarros. Nor did he have any intention of confiding in her as to the unacceptable—and persistent—sexual advances of his father's second wife which, when discovered, had resulted in his father believing her claims that she hadn't wanted to tell him but Raphael had been pestering her to have sex with him for months behind his back. It was perhaps that last detail that hurt Raphael the most. That, at the time, his father had chosen to believe his wife's version of events rather than that of his own son…

Raphael looked at Beth coolly. 'Perhaps because I do not make a habit of confiding my…personal family business with people I have only just met.'

Beth drew her breath in sharply. Was that how Raphael thought of her, as merely a person he had just met? And why should he think of her in any other way? Because they had shared a few kisses and intimacies earlier this evening? Albeit intimacies that Beth had never allowed with another man…

What had happened between the two of them earlier might have been unique in Beth's limited physical experience, but it certainly wasn't in Raphael's. In fact, the opposite, if his expertise in that area was any indication. It was also an incident he had told her he would rather they both forgot…

'You're right, Raphael, this steak really is inedible.' She gave him a tight smile as she stood up. 'I think I'll go to bed now. I'm feeling rather tired after all the travelling today. Leave all this.' She waved a hand towards the mess on the table. 'I'll clear it away in the morning.'

Raphael recognised the lie for what it was. 'You have not eaten anything.'

'I'm no longer hungry.' Her eyes flashed darkly as she looked challengingly across the kitchen at him.

He scowled darkly. 'Why are you making such a fuss over something that is basically none of your business?'

Her chin rose as she gave a humourless smile. 'Glad to see you haven't lost your brutal honesty—in regard to some subjects, at least!'

Raphael winced. 'It was not my intention to be brutal—'

'Then I'll know to stay well out of your way when it is,' Beth came back with hard derision. 'What time are we leaving for London in the morning?'

He frowned his displeasure with the change of subject. 'I thought seven-thirty.'

'I should make it seven o'clock.' She frowned. 'The London traffic can be awful at that time of the morning.'

'I will inform Edward,' he confirmed tersely.

The golden swathe of her hair fell forward over her shoulders as Beth nodded. 'Goodnight, Raphael, and don't work too hard,' she added dryly before leaving.

'Goodnight, Beth…' Raphael murmured softly as he stared at the doorway Beth had disappeared through.

As he continued to wonder, long after Beth must have reached her bedroom, exactly how they were going to proceed during the long days or weeks ahead.

Having decided, after that unforgivable incident in the gym earlier this evening, that he had to maintain his distance from Beth in future, Raphael now deeply regretted having told her the little about his family that he had.

Regretted having ever met the disturbing Beth Blake at all...

CHAPTER SIX

'I'VE NEVER SEEN anyone so dark and broodingly gorgeous in my entire life!'

'Gorgeous? The man is sex on two long, perfectly muscled legs!'

'And did you see the size of those shoulders…?'

'It's the size of his feet you have to look at, silly.'

'Going to let me in on the secret, ladies?' Beth had strolled over to look enquiringly at the three giggling women who worked in her office as they gathered conspiratorially around the coffee machine during the morning break.

'I can do better than that. Come and look out of the window!' Kathy grabbed hold of her arm and dragged her across the room to where the windows looked directly down into the street three floors below. 'See!' she announced triumphantly. 'He was standing right there when we all came into work this morning.'

Beth should have guessed what—and who!—was causing this uproar amongst her female work colleagues. Raphael Cordoba stood across the street, leaning conspicuously on the wall behind him, looking gorgeous in another one of those dark three-piece suits, and wearing those familiar mirrored sunglasses as a shield to the expression in his eyes, if not to his other more than obvious physical attributes.

Physical attributes Beth's female work colleagues were obviously all agog over!

Not surprisingly, considering those dark and dangerous good looks, and that air of the stalking predator that he wore like a second skin.

Beth had deliberately arranged things so that she arrived at work earlier than anyone else this morning, in an effort to avoid being seen getting out of the chauffeur-driven limousine. Only for Raphael to then announce that he intended coming into the building with her, and spending the day standing beside her desk. She had managed to talk him out of that one, with the compromise that he would wait outside and she wouldn't attempt to leave the building. But the hope that none of her work colleagues would notice the highly noticeable Raphael Cordoba standing outside on the pavement had obviously been a futile one.

'Isn't he just the most sexy man you've ever set eyes on?' Emma joined the two of them at the window.

'If you like tall, dark, and brooding, yes,' Beth agreed lightly.

'What woman in her right mind doesn't appreciate tall, dark and brooding?' Amy moved to stand at Beth's other side. 'He's been standing out there for at least two hours now. I wonder what he's waiting for?'

Beth had two choices at this point in the conversation. She could deny all knowledge of Raphael—which, considering he would no doubt approach and talk to her when she left the building later on today, making it obvious the two of them knew each other, probably wasn't the best move!—or she could admit to knowing him, if not the real reason he stood outside watching the comings and going into the building so intently.

She went with the second option. 'He's waiting for me, actually,' she announced casually, wincing slightly as the other three women immediately all turned to look at her with wide, incredulous, and envious eyes, respectively. 'Raphael drove me into work this morning, and we're having lunch together, so he decided to hang around until then rather than drive home and then come back into town again later.' All true—apart from the bit about the two of them having lunch together!

'Raphael?' Emma prompted breathlessly as she turned back to look out of the window.

'Raphael Cordoba,' Beth supplied reluctantly, wondering if she hadn't just made this situation even more difficult. If that was possible, of course. 'He's Argentinian.'

'You only spent a week in Argentina and you still managed to bring that hunk back with you?' The forthright Kathy stared at her.

'Well…yes.' Beth winced. 'We met through mutual friends, and he decided to—to come back to England with me for a while.' Again, all true—apart from the one little fact Beth *hadn't* mentioned, which was that Raphael was here as her bodyguard and not her boyfriend.

Not that the words 'boyfriend' and 'Raphael Cordoba' could ever be put together in the same sentence anyway!

Raphael might only be ten years older than Beth in calendar years, but he was years older than that in sophistication and experience. Most especially physical experience…

The latter was something that Beth had definitely been made fully aware of the previous evening!

'He drove you into work this morning?' Tall, blonde, beautiful, and extremely nice Amy was the one to latch onto that comment.

Beth's cheeks instantly coloured self-consciously at what that obviously implied. 'Yes, he did.'

'And do the size of his feet— Ouch!' Emma complained as Kathy dug her in the ribs with her elbow. 'I was only going to ask!'

'I believe we all know what you were going to ask.' Kathy chuckled softly. 'And I think it's bad enough that we've all been standing here drooling over Beth's boyfriend, without making the situation worse by asking her highly personal questions.'

'I agree.' Amy nodded briskly even as she gave Beth an apologetic glance. 'Coffee break's over, ladies, time to go back to work.'

Beth breathed an inward sigh of relief as they all turned and returned to their respective desks.

At the same time as she realised that her explanation for Raphael's presence outside meant they might not have been going to have lunch together today but that they certainly were now!

'I thought you said it was your intention to have lunch at your desk.' Raphael's comment was cut short as Beth, having linked her arm with his, now rested her hands against his chest before moving up on tiptoe and lightly brushing the softness of her lips against his.

She moved away abruptly. 'Would you just walk?' she instructed between the gritted teeth that were obviously meant to resemble a smile.

Raphael's feet remained firmly planted on the pavement. 'Walk where?'

'This way,' Beth hissed even as she waved to a tall and beautiful blonde woman on the other side of the street. 'Just start walking and I'll tell you when to stop.' She dragged him along beside her as she stomped off down the street.

'It is too much to ask for an explanation as to your

strange behaviour, I suppose?' Raphael prompted dryly as he fell into easy step beside her.

Brown eyes flashed Beth's irritation as she spared him an impatient glance. 'Do you have to wear those sunglasses all the time? The sun isn't even shining today!'

Raphael reached up and removed the offending glasses before placing them in the breast pocket of his jacket. 'Better?'

'Much!' Which was a total lie, when Beth found being the sole focus of those piercing blue eyes so totally unnerving. Just as she was desperately trying, after Kathy's risqué comments earlier, not to glance down and admire Raphael's size-twelve feet...

'Enough so that you will now answer my question?'

She sighed heavily as she glanced quickly away from his feet. 'The people I work with all think that the two of us are having lunch together.'

Raphael raised surprised brows. 'And why would they think that?'

'Because I told them that we were.'

'Why?'

Another one of those questions Beth would rather not answer. After the put-down she had received from Raphael the night before she would rather not spend any more time alone with him at all. Or be so aware now of the muscled tautness of his arm beneath her fingertips!

'Oh, come on, Raphael, you've been standing out here for hours now, surely you must need a toilet break, if nothing else,' she taunted in an effort to hide that awareness. 'Unless, of course, your training in that special unit in the army involved bladder control!'

His mouth tightened. 'It did.'

Beth shot him a frustrated glance. 'Well, that's just too

bad, because whether you're hungry or not, in need of the loo or not, we are having lunch together.'

'Because the people you work with are expecting us to do so...'

'Yes!'

'Ah, I think I understand now.' Raphael's expression cleared. 'You have possibly told your work colleagues that the two of us are...involved, as a way of explaining my presence here today?'

'Well, aren't you the smart ar—er—alec.' Beth frowned up at him.

Raphael chuckled softly. 'Purely a guess on my part.'

'Yes. Well.' She frowned her irritation. 'It happens to be the correct one. And I'm not at all happy about it, so you can take that damned grin off your dark and broodingly gorgeous face!'

His brows rose higher. 'I am assuming that is the opinion of one of your work colleagues and not how you personally think of me?'

'You would assume correctly,' Beth assured him evenly; how and what she thought of Raphael Cordoba was no one else's business but her own—it certainly wasn't something she intended sharing with Raphael himself. Again... Because Beth had no doubts that the previous evening she had revealed exactly how physically attractive she found this man. 'I don't suppose it's occurred to you that I might already have a boyfriend, who isn't going to be at all happy about my having claimed the two of us are now involved?'

'And do you?' The expression on that 'dark and broodingly gorgeous' face remained coolly impassive.

A reaction that irritated Beth intensely. 'None of your damned business!'

'But it is my business, Beth,' Raphael grated. 'Everything about you is now my business. And if there is a man in your life then he will need to be—'

'Vetted?' she suggested dryly.

'Investigated,' Raphael corrected stiffly.

'And how do you go about doing that, Raphael?' she taunted. 'Do you check the man's background—family, friends, place of work, previous relationships—before deciding whether or not he passes the Raphael Cordoba test?'

A nerve pulsed in the tightness of his jaw. 'I cannot say I have ever been in quite this position before.'

'But no doubt you've had to carry out such investigations into the women Cesar has been involved with in the past?'

His mouth thinned. 'I will not discuss Cesar's private life with you or anyone else.'

Beth's initial irritation had faded to be replaced with the usual need she felt to tease this coldly remote man. 'Frightened I might tell Grace what a bad boy Cesar was before he met her?'

He looked down at her reprovingly. 'Beth—'

'I'm just joking, Raphael!' She chuckled throatily. 'Grace loves Cesar so much she's only interested in their future together, not his past.'

'Which is exactly as it should be.' He nodded tersely. 'Did you have somewhere specific in mind for lunch or are we just going to keep walking about aimlessly for the next hour?' he added impatiently.

'I've booked a table for us at Ronaldo's. I chose an Italian restaurant because I don't know of any Argentinian ones,' she added dismissively.

'Italian is fine.'

'It's a very good restaurant,' Beth assured him. 'Quite a lot of the editors use it when they take authors out for lunch.'

'And is one of those editors the "boyfriend" you suggested might take exception to the two of us being seen together?'

She grinned up at him. 'Now, that would be interesting, don't you think?'

'I believe it would be typical of you rather than interesting.'

She gave a mock pout. 'You know, Raphael, my feelings could be hurt by remarks like that one.'

He snorted dismissively. 'Somehow I doubt that very much!'

'Because you don't believe I have feelings that could be hurt?'

He gave a derisive shake of his head. 'Because I believe you would enjoy seeing two men fighting over you.'

Beth's breath caught in her throat. 'You would fight another man over me?'

'Only if he represented a threat to your well being.'

'Oh.'

Raphael raised mocking brows. 'Did you expect me to say something else?'

'Obviously not,' she muttered.

'You perhaps thought, after I made the mistake of kissing you last night, that I now have a personal interest in you?' There was no missing the sharp edge to his tone.

Beth's cheeks felt hot, both at the reminder of those kisses—and the fact that Raphael obviously thought of them as a mistake. 'Now you're being deliberately nasty.'

'Which, contrarily, somehow seems to give you satisfaction?'

In a strange way it did. But only because Beth was finding she preferred to have some sort of reaction from Raphael rather than none; Mr Iceman of the drive into town early this morning wasn't acceptable to her at all.

But she certainly hadn't wanted to be reminded of their time in the gym together last night. Or to hear that it had meant nothing to Raphael—he had made that more than obvious enough at the time!

She deliberately changed the subject. 'I hope you like Italian food.'

'Does it matter one way or the other?' he derided dryly.

'Raphael—'

'I apologise,' he bit out stiffly. 'That was rude of me. Yes, I enjoy Italian food.'

'But maybe you would prefer not to be eating it with me?'

How was Raphael supposed to answer that question? On the one hand, he should not even be contemplating sitting down and eating lunch with the person he was here to protect. On the other, Raphael very much liked the idea of having lunch with Beth; it certainly couldn't help but be an improvement on the dinner they had shared together the previous evening!

Speaking of which… 'Kevin Maddox is going to try and organise a temporary cook for us at the estate in the next day or so, but if we both eat a hot meal now then we can perhaps manage with a snack when we return there later this evening.' Raphael chose not to answer her question at all.

'Oh, very practical, Raphael,' Beth came back dryly.

Raphael shrugged. 'I am a practical man.'

She gave a wistful sigh. 'Yes, you are.'

He moved forward to open the door of the restaurant for her. 'You make that sound like a reason for criticism?'

'A little spontaneity would be nice on occasion,' she dismissed lightly, having given her name to the waiter before he took them to the reserved table near the window.

Raphael followed slowly behind her, knowing that spontaneity was responsible for his having crossed the line the previous evening, when he had kissed and caressed Beth. A lapse for which he had paid dearly when he went to his bedroom later that evening, only to lie awake in his bed long into the early hours of this morning as he remembered the feel and taste of Beth, and the perfection of her breasts tipped with those rose-coloured and responsive nipples that he had lathed and suckled with his tongue and mouth.

Madre mia, he was hard again just thinking about it!

'Raphael?'

He brought his thoughts under strict control as he took his own seat opposite Beth's at the table—if nothing else the red-and-white-checked tablecloth served to hide the fierce throb of his erection!

Raphael had been totally disconcerted earlier when Beth came out of the building and moved up on tiptoe to kiss him on the lips—he probably had that momentary confusion to thank for not kissing her back, and so making the situation worse, before she explained exactly why she had kissed him. He hadn't been immune to the warmth of her hand resting on his arm as they walked to the restaurant together, either. And he was still aware that he hadn't received an answer from Beth as to whether or not she currently had a boyfriend. Which, for some reason, continued to irritate him…

Boyfriend or not, the fact that he now had a raging erection just thinking of making love to Beth told Raphael that, from a practical perspective, he wasn't the right person to be in charge of Beth's protection, that his emotions weren't detached enough for his reactions to be as cool and precise as they needed to be. Although how Raphael would go about explaining that lack of detachment to Cesar, without revealing the extent of last night's lapse, he had no idea—

'Have you spoken to Cesar today?'

Raphael looked sharply across the table at Beth as she seemed to guess some of his thoughts, the frown easing from his brow as he knew by the blandness of her expression that she was merely attempting to make polite conversation. 'Late last night,' he answered tersely.

'And?' Beth picked one of the bread sticks out of the tall glass in the middle of the table and began to chew on it.

'And he sent you his regards and Grace's love,' Raphael drawled dryly even as his gaze was drawn to watching those tiny white teeth as they nibbled delicately on the bread stick. The same delectably delicate nibbles he could all too easily imagine her making on his cock before she took him deep—

'Which you obviously forgot to pass on to me this morning?'

Raphael gave a shrug as he forced himself to relax back against the chair. Not so easy to do when Bath was now sucking on that bread stick! And being deliberately provocative? No, the distracted expression on her face, and the frown between her eyes, told him that Beth had absolutely no idea how sensually provocative she was being at this moment.

'You were not exactly talkative on the drive into London earlier,' he rasped hoarsely. 'And our conversation this past few minutes has been on other things.'

'You weren't exactly Mr Chatterbox yourself. Besides, I'm not a morning person.' Beth shrugged.

'I will try to remember that.'

Beth could think of only one circumstance under which Raphael would need to remember that—and after hearing him describe kissing her as being a 'mistake', she very much doubted *that* particular situation was ever going to arise! 'Grace and I have always had an agreement, in that she doesn't talk to me in the morning, and in return I don't growl at her.'

Raphael continued to look at her for several moments, as if he had something on his mind, something he wanted to say to her, before obviously deciding otherwise as he scowled darkly before giving a dismissive shake of his head and glancing down at the menu. 'What do you recommend?'

Beth breathed easily for the first time in several minutes. 'It's all good,' she dismissed lightly before turning her attention to studying her own menu. Anything was better than sitting here ogling this 'dark and broodingly gorgeous' man, moreover a man who had made it patently obvious that her company irritated him at best and outright annoyed him at worst!

Raphael couldn't remember ever having had lunch alone with a woman before. The occasional dinner with a woman, prior to going to bed with her, but he had always considered that lunch was for conversation and couples who were something more to one another than temporary bed-partners.

Consequently eating lunch with a woman was a novel experience for him. Eating lunch with the outspoken Beth Blake was, he very quickly learnt, a uniquely entertaining one. She conversed—and predictably had strong opinions!—on a variety of subjects: world politics, new fashions, the wave of eBooks currently taking the publishing world by storm, holidays they had both taken, the quality or otherwise of the latest film releases…and in return Raphael found himself comfortable giving his own opinion on those same subjects.

The food was, as Beth had claimed, also of a very high standard, although they had both preferred, as they had to return to work within the hour, to drink sparkling water with their food rather than wine.

'My treat,' Beth assured Raphael as the waiter placed the bill on their table at the end of the meal.

He frowned his displeasure with that arrangement. 'It is the man who usually pays.'

She gave him a teasing glance as she placed the money on the table beside the bill. 'For the bill, or emotionally?'

'In my experience, both.'

She smiled derisively. 'Did someone forget to tell you that this is the twenty-first century, and that consequently women now consider it their right to invite a man out to lunch, and pay for it, if they want to?'

'And a lot of those men are far from comfortable with twenty-first-century…customs.'

Beth chuckled softly at his typically Raphael opinion. 'I'm quite happy to let you invite me out and pay next time if you want to.'

'Next time?' Raphael questioned frowningly. Was lunch with Beth to become a habit rather than the exception? Along with the throbbing erection he had continued to suffer throughout the meal? 'I am sure your boyfriend would have reason to be displeased if we were to lunch together a second time…' Raphael stood up to move round the table and pull back Beth's chair for her.

She gave another chuckle as the two of them walked to the door of the restaurant. 'There is no boyfriend, Raphael.'

'You only implied as much in order to annoy me,' he guessed dryly as he opened that door.

She quirked blond brows as she paused in the doorway. 'Why should I ever have imagined you would have any feelings on the subject one way or the other?'

Why indeed? The fact that Raphael *had* been annoyed only made his irritation all the deeper now. 'I would, as you said, have needed to investigate this man before the two of you went out together again.'

'That doesn't answer my question, Raphael…'

No, it didn't. And Raphael wasn't about to, either.

Because he didn't have an answer. None that was acceptable, anyway. To himself. Last night—and his arousal today, just thinking about making love with Beth last night!—had proved how much he desired her. But he was also starting to respect as well as like her, to admire her intelligence. Far too much than was wise, given their present circumstances. 'An answer is unnecessary when there is no boyfriend,' he rasped.

She put the strap of her bag over her shoulder before continuing outside. 'Still, I might have found it interesting to know what the answer was going to be,' she murmured with what sounded like disappointment.

Raphael's breath caught in his throat, both at Beth's close proximity, and the insidious and erotic smell of her perfume; an arousing combination of that lightly floral scent and the desirable woman who was wearing that perfume.

He straightened at the same time as he gave a dismissive shake of his head. 'I believe your lunch hour is over.'

Oh, yes, Beth's lunch hour was over. And it had been a surprisingly enjoyable hour, interesting conversation in the company of an intelligent and handsome man who also made her heart beat faster just to look at him. An hour when Beth had also learnt much more about Raphael than before: his likes and dislikes, his view on what was happening in the world, the books he liked to read, actors he admired, plays and films he had enjoyed attending. Although he had continued to refuse to be drawn on any remarks regarding family, his own or the Navarros…

It had also been an hour when Beth had noted that several other women in the restaurant had obviously liked looking at Raphael as much as she did. An occurrence Beth found she hadn't enjoyed at all!

Not that Raphael had seemed in the least aware of any of those surreptitious female glances being sent his way, his attention centered completely on Beth and their conversation.

His professional attention.

Because that was all Beth was, or ever could be, to Raphael: just another person he was employed to protect.

What a depressing thought!

'You are very quiet.'

Beth sent Raphael a teasing glance as they walked back to her office. 'Stimulating conversation and delicious food always do that to me.'

He arched dark brows. 'That is two more things I have learnt about you today.'

Her brows rose. 'Two?'

He nodded. 'You are not a morning person, and you go silent when stimulated and satiated.'

Beth felt her cheeks warm as she corrected him, 'With conversation and food.'

'Ah, yes, with conversation and food...'

Beth's gaze sharpened. 'If I didn't know better, Raphael, I would think you were flirting with me!'

He gave a hard smile as he shrugged. 'I am merely practising my role as your presumed boyfriend for when we return to your office building.'

Was he?

And were those feelings of disappointment Beth was experiencing, at the thought that was Raphael's only reason for being flirtatious with her?

Get a grip, she told herself sternly. Raphael wouldn't be here in England with her at all if Cesar hadn't arranged for him to accompany her. If Cesar hadn't arranged for Raphael to accompany Gabriela Navarro; a young woman with a family and lifestyle that remained totally alien to Beth.

'Good enough.' She nodded dismissively as she stepped out more decisively in the direction of her office.

A brisk and no-nonsense attitude, which in no way prepared Beth for Raphael coming to a halt outside the building where she worked a few minutes later, that piercing blue gaze holding hers captive as he took her into his arms and kissed her!

CHAPTER SEVEN

RAPHAEL HAD GIVEN in to the need he had been suffering under for the past hour: to kiss this woman. The initial arousal an hour ago, as he had watched Beth nibbling on bread sticks, had only increased as he had been unable to look away as he watched each morsel of food passing those full and sensual lips.

He gave a groan now and deepened the kiss as Beth parted those lips beneath his, her hands sliding up his chest and over the width of his shoulders, before her fingers became entangled in the short hair at his nape as she curved her body into his.

A response that caused Raphael's already pulsing arousal to become even harder and more insistent, an insistence that demanded he take this woman...now!

A realisation that shot such a wave of foreboding through him that he abruptly ended the kiss to put Beth firmly away from him before his hands dropped back to his sides, his lids narrowing as he looked down at her warily.

Beth returned that gaze for several dazed seconds, her eyes a dark and slightly unfocused black. 'What just happened?'

Raphael wished he knew the answer to that. Or did he? This attraction he felt for Beth Blake was becoming

OFFICIAL OPINION POLL

Dear Reader,

Since you are a book enthusiast, we would like to know what you think.

Inside you will find a short Opinion Poll. Please participate in our poll by sharing your opinion on 3 subjects that are very important to all of us.

To thank you for your participation, we would like to send you **2 FREE BOOKS** and **2 FREE GIFTS!**

Please enjoy them with our compliments.

Sincerely,

Pam Powers

YOUR OPINION POLL
THANK-YOU FREE GIFTS INCLUDE:

▶ **2 HARLEQUIN PRESENTS® BOOKS**

▶ **2 LOVELY SURPRISE GIFTS**

OFFICIAL OPINION POLL

YOUR OPINION COUNTS!
Please check TRUE or FALSE below to express your opinion about the following statements:

Q1 Do you believe in "true love"?

"TRUE LOVE HAPPENS ONLY ONCE IN A LIFETIME."
○ TRUE
○ FALSE

Q2 Do you think marriage has any value in today's world?

"YOU CAN BE TOTALLY COMMITTED TO SOMEONE WITHOUT BEING MARRIED."
○ TRUE
○ FALSE

Q3 What kind of books do you enjoy?

"A GREAT NOVEL MUST HAVE A HAPPY ENDING."
○ TRUE
○ FALSE

YES! I have placed my sticker in the space provided below. Please send me the **2 FREE books** and **2 FREE gifts** for which I qualify. I understand that I am under no obligation to purchase anything further, as explained on the back of this card.

❏ I prefer the regular-print edition
106/306 HDL FVPU

❏ I prefer the larger-print edition
176/376 HDL FVPU

FIRST NAME

LAST NAME

ADDRESS

APT.#

CITY

STATE/PROV.

ZIP/POSTAL CODE

Offer limited to one per household and not applicable to series that subscriber is currently receiving.
Your Privacy—The Harlequin® Reader Service is committed to protecting your privacy. Our Privacy Policy is available online at www.ReaderService.com or upon request from the Harlequin Reader Service. We make a portion of our mailing list available to reputable third parties that offer products we believe may interest you. If you prefer that we not exchange your name with third parties, or if you wish to clarify or modify your communication preferences, please visit us at www.ReaderService.com/consumerchoice or write to us at Harlequin Reader Service Preference Service, P.O. Box 9062, Buffalo, NY 14269. Include your complete name and address.

Printed in the U.S.A.
© 2012 HARLEQUIN ENTERPRISES LIMITED.

If offer card is missing write to: Harlequin Reader Service, P.O. Box 1867, Buffalo NY 14240-1867 or visit: www.ReaderService.com

BUSINESS REPLY MAIL

FIRST-CLASS MAIL   PERMIT NO. 717   BUFFALO, NY

POSTAGE WILL BE PAID BY ADDRESSEE

HARLEQUIN READER SERVICE
PO BOX 1341
BUFFALO NY 14240-8571

NO POSTAGE
NECESSARY
IF MAILED
IN THE
UNITED STATES

something of a problem for him. 'We have an audience,' he explained harshly.

Beth glanced dazedly over one of Raphael's broad shoulders to see several of her work colleagues—including a smilingly indulgent Amy!—looking at the two of them curiously as Beth was very soundly kissed—and returning the passion of that kiss!—outside her office building.

She pulled back abruptly, her eyes accusing as she glared up at Raphael. 'I don't enjoy being used!'

He frowned darkly. 'I believe you were the one who chose to tell your work colleagues that the two of us are involved as a way of explaining my presence here.'

Beth eyed him impatiently. 'There's a difference between my having to tell them that and having you make love to me in the middle of a public street.'

Raphael looked down at her for several moments, knowing that he shouldn't have kissed Beth just now, and feeling angry with himself for further complicating an already complicated situation.

'As I am sure you are well aware, I had not even begun to make love to you...' he rasped harshly.

Colour flooded her cheeks. 'You know exactly what I meant!'

Yes, Raphael knew exactly what Beth meant. Just as he knew the accusation was perfectly justified, and that a few minutes more of kissing Beth and he would have totally ignored—forgotten!—the fact that he was here in England to act as her protector rather than her lover.

He drew himself up stiffly. 'It will not happen again.'

Beth drew in a sharp breath at the coldness of Raphael's tone, at the same time as she inwardly acknowledged she was more affected by being kissed by him than she should have been. Or wanted to be. 'Just—just because the two of us kissed yesterday, doesn't mean I intend to let you make a habit of it,' she warned exasperatedly at the same time as her heart skipped a beat—several beats!—just at the thought of being kissed by Raphael again.

'I have said it will not happen again,' he rasped icily.

'And I bet you're a man who never breaks his word, huh?' she came back scornfully.

His eyes glittered with that same coldness. 'I am a man who *tries* never to break his word, yes.'

Beth grimaced. 'Well, in this case I advise that you do more than try!'

'Or?'

Beth was incensed by the glint of mocking humour she detected in those piercing blue eyes. 'Or you can go to hell along with my big brother—' She broke off in shocked surprise as she realised that for the first time she had referred to Cesar Navarro as her brother. As if she was finally starting to accept the concept that she just might be Gabriela Navarro, after all... 'It's time I went back to work,' she bit out abruptly, her expression bleak, and her gaze no longer meeting Raphael's. 'And no doubt you will continue your vigil throughout the afternoon?' she rallied enough to mock dryly.

'No doubt.' Raphael nodded slowly, ignoring Beth's outburst in favour of recognising that she had just referred to Cesar as her brother, and feeling a certain amount of relief at that knowledge. No matter how much she would prefer it not to be the truth, it would seem that, inwardly at least, Beth was starting to accept her destiny might be as Gabriela Navarro.

Which might be as well, when Raphael might, hoped, to be in possession of confirmation of that fact later on today...

'This morning I now understand, but your silence this evening is very...un-Beth-like.'

Beth turned from gazing out of the window to look at Raphael instead as he once again sat in the front of the limousine beside Edward. A limousine that had, thankfully, been parked around the corner from her office building when Beth left work half an hour ago. At Raphael's request? Out of consideration for the fact that he knew Beth didn't want any of her work colleagues to see her getting into the back of a chauffeur-driven limousine? Probably.

To say Beth had been disturbed by that unexpected kiss earlier—no matter what reason Raphael claimed for instigating it!—would be an understatement. So much so that she had found herself wandering over to the windows once or twice during the afternoon—or it just might have been a dozen times!—and gazing down at him in frowning confusion.

Not only did his dark and brooding good looks make her heart beat faster, but she was also drawn to the quiet strength Raphael exuded, an unspoken assurance that no harm would come to anyone he cared about—or, as in Beth's case, who was in his care—on his watch. It was a strange, and yet intriguing, combination; dangerous sensuality alongside that quiet and yet totally reassuring strength.

An irresistible combination as far as Beth was concerned!

Which, in the circumstances, was pretty stupid of her...

She gave him a tight, humourless smile. 'I thought it was a woman's prerogative to be unpredictable? As well as irrational and unreasonable? Edward obviously understands that, if you don't,' she added dryly as she heard the chauffeur chuckle softly.

'I'm a married man, miss. What else need I say?' The chauffeur continued to chuckle indulgently.

'And, as a married man, you find this uncertainty of

mood acceptable?' Raphael gave the other man a searching glance.

'It is what it is, Mr Cordoba.' Edward shrugged. 'Can't live with 'em, can't live without 'em. Besides, it's the unpredictable element of our women that keeps a man on his toes.'

'If you say so...' Raphael murmured slowly.

Beth would have laughed at the doubtful expression on Raphael's face—if she hadn't been reeling slightly from Edward's comment of 'our women'! Because she wasn't, and never would be, Raphael Cordoba's 'woman'.

Did she want to be?

Her life felt too complicated at this moment for Beth to be sure what she wanted. From anyone or anything.

'You sound less than impressed, Raphael,' she drawled dryly.

He arched one dark brow. 'At least you are talking now.'

Beth gave a rueful smile. 'I thought talking was another thing we women did too much of.'

His mouth twisted derisively. 'I believe it is the conversations that begin with "the two of us need to talk" that are apt to send shivers down a man's spine!'

'And do you speak from personal experience?' she came back sweetly—at the same time as Beth realised she didn't like even the thought of Raphael ever being so deeply involved with a woman that there had ever been the need for one of those conversations. That she actually felt *jealous* of the women from Raphael's past. And possibly his present? Because they might have discussed whether or not Beth had anyone else in her life right now, but the subject of Raphael's past or present relationships had never entered their conversation.

'No, I do not, thank goodness.' Raphael's dismissive reply was no help in answering that question, either.

'I think I'll close my eyes and have a sleep for the rest of the journey,' Beth muttered before leaning her head back and closing her eyes, effectively shutting out the sight of Raphael if not her complete awareness of him.

Raphael frowned as he looked at Beth's closed lids. The eyes were the windows to the soul, he had heard. And it could not have been more true where Beth was concerned. Those dark brown eyes, fiery with anger one moment, gleaming with laughter the next, and then dark and seductive during arousal, were a complete reflection of Beth's emotions.

Emotions Raphael had no chance of reading when her lids were closed.

Deliberately so, he believed.

Because, for all of her outward bravado, there was another part of Beth that she kept completely hidden. The part deep inside her that was confused and hurting at the mere thought of being Gabriela Navarro rather than Beth Blake.

Raphael had no doubts that her need not to share those emotions with him was because Beth considered him to be another one of the people conspiring to prove that was exactly who she was.

And she would be right...

Rodney was once again waiting for them in the cavernous hallway of Cesar's mansion house when they arrived back at the estate half an hour or so later. One look at the bland expression on Rodney's face as he gave Raphael a brief nod in answer to his silently enquiring glance was enough to set all of Beth's alarm bells ringing.

'What's happened?' she prompted warily.

Rodney looked at her blankly. '"Happened", Miss Navarro?'

The 'Miss Navarro' just made those alarm bells jangle all the louder.

'Happened,' she echoed grimly. 'And don't try and tell me that nothing has,' she warned as the security man opened his mouth to reply, 'because I won't believe you. Either of you,' she added with a pointed glance at Raphael.

Raphael's expression remained coolly aloof. 'I am sure, after your hard day at work, that you must now wish to freshen up and change before dinner.'

Beth set her feet more firmly on the tiled hallway. 'Not until I know what's going on.'

Raphael's mouth tightened with impatience at the look of stubbornness on Beth's face as she looked up at him challengingly. 'You will be informed of what is going on after I have spoken to Rodney. Alone,' he added tightly as Beth's expression now set in mutinous lines.

She gave a slow and stiff shake of her head. 'That isn't good enough.'

'Nevertheless—'

'Raphael, unless I'm mistaken, it's my life, and my future, the two of you are going to be discussing!' Her brown eyes flashed darkly with anger.

Yes, it was, and Raphael had no doubts, having come to know Beth much better these last few days, that her present anger was a shield to those other, bewildered and frightened emotions she kept locked inside her, rather than anger itself.

His expression gentled slightly. 'And if I were to promise to inform you immediately, if what Rodney is about to report is of relevance to you?' Raphael winced slightly as he sensed, rather than saw, the way Rodney stiffened.

Implying the investigations the other man had carried out today, under Raphael's instruction, were indeed significant…

Beth was still eyeing the two of them with suspicion. 'I have your word on that?'

Raphael nodded stiffly. 'I have just said so.'

She drew in a deep and shaky breath. 'Okay.' She nodded tersely. 'You know where my bedroom is,' she added with a return of her usual derisive humour, before sending him a mocking smile and moving lithely up the wide staircase.

Raphael ignored the jibe as he waited until Beth had disappeared down one of the hallways at the top of the stairs before turning back to the other man. 'I take it that your visit to the parish of Stopley in Surrey proved fruitful?'

'Oh, yes.' Rodney's stiff smile of confirmation was more of a humourless grimace.

A grimness echoed in Raphael's own mood as the two men retired to the privacy of Cesar's study for the rest of their discussion.

A discussion Raphael had no doubts he would shortly be relating to Beth.

Waiting to see if Raphael would come up to her bedroom was a little like being in a dentist's waiting room—and just as painful. That Rodney had something of import to relate to Raphael, she had no doubts. Something of import to her...

In an effort to keep herself busy Beth finished unpacking the last of her clothes from her suitcase, putting them on hangers before placing them in the wardrobe, and then going through to the adjoining bathroom to take a shower and changing out of the business suit and blouse she had worn to work.

None of which helped to settle the fluttering sensation in her chest and the butterflies in her stomach. At this rate, all this suspense and tension were going to give her a heart attack, and then it wouldn't matter to anyone who she was: Beth Blake or Gabriela Navarro.

And no doubt, despite all of her denials, she was going to find out the answer to that soon enough…

Even so, Beth was slightly taken aback to leave the steam-filled bathroom, wearing only a towel wrapped about her, to find Raphael waiting for her in her bedroom!

His back was turned towards her as he stood outlined in front of one of the two windows, staring out into the wooded grounds at the rear of the house. Those same woods where Beth knew Grace had jokingly suggested Cesar might like to have her buried after one of her sister's more outspoken exchanges with him!

None of which was of the least importance right now, when Raphael could have only one purpose for being here…

Beth moved further into the bedroom. 'I take it you have bad news,' she prompted sharply.

He turned slowly to face her, taking in her appearance with a single glance of narrowed blue eyes, before a shutter came down over those piercing orbs. 'Surely that depends upon your perspective on the situation?'

She gave a derisive snort. 'I think we both know my perspective on this situation!'

Raphael frowned darkly. 'Perhaps you would care to dress before we talk?'

Beth raised one blond brow. 'Is that going to make what you're about to tell me any more acceptable?'

He grimaced. 'Probably not.'

'Then I don't think I'll bother.' Beth might feel uncomfortable wearing only a towel in Raphael's presence, but at the same time she could see it was a discomfort he also shared. A discomfort she felt put them on a more equal footing—and she needed all the leverage available to her when in the presence of this imposing Argentinian! 'Well?' she prompted when he remained silent.

Raphael sighed, knowing by the light of battle he could see in Beth's eyes—when he at last managed to drag his gaze away from the wild tumble of her blond hair and the visible swell of her creamy breasts above the dark green towel that barely covered the tops of her long and shapely legs!—that she was not about to make the next few minutes easy for him.

Any more than they were going to be easy ones for her...

His mouth thinned. 'Our investigations these past few days established that James and Carla Lawrence resided in the Parish of Stopley in Surrey, before they later moved to the house in Kent, where you also resided until their deaths eighteen years ago.'

The tightness in Beth's chest increased, her breathing so shallow it barely existed at all. 'And?'

Raphael's expression was pained. 'I believe we discussed a scenario some days ago regarding the proof you felt you needed in order to believe the Navarros' claim?'

Beth felt the colour drain from her cheeks, and she stumbled slightly as she moved to drop down weakly onto the side of the bed. 'A gravestone, dated twenty-one years ago, with the name of two-year-old Elizabeth Lawrence etched into it...' she related dully.

'Yes.'

Her eyes widened. 'Rodney found it?'

'Yes. Beth—'

'Don't, Raphael!' She held up a hand to ward him away from touching her as he would have moved to her side, unable to so much as look at him as the full shock of what he was saying embedded itself deep inside her.

There was a grave.

With the name of two-year-old Elizabeth Lawrence etched into it.

With *her* name etched into it.

Except it wasn't her name.

How could it be, when two-year-old Elizabeth Lawrence had died twenty-one years ago?

And two-year-old Gabriela Navarro had been taken, abducted, to take that other little girl's place, in the Lawrences' home as well as their hearts?

And yes, it was the evidence that Beth had said she needed, if she was ever to believe the claim of Carlos and Esther Navarro that she was their missing daughter.

Except it wasn't.

Not really.

Oh, Beth had verbally denied being Gabriela Navarro, and had physically removed herself from the Navarro family's vicinity, but deep inside her Beth had known that type of blood test was never wrong, that her likeness to Esther Navarro was too startling to be a coincidence, that the photographs of two-year-old Gabriela Navarro and two-year-old Beth were identical—a likeness, and photographs, that were the main reason for Grace having initially jumped to the conclusion that she had! And now—now there was a grave, with Elizabeth Lawrence's name on it—

'Beth?'

She raised bleak brown eyes to look at Raphael as he watched her closely from across the bedroom. 'I'm really her.' It was a statement rather than a question.

'Yes.'

She moistened the dryness of her lips with the tip of her tongue. 'Do the Navarros know? About Elizabeth Lawrence's grave?'

'Not yet.' Raphael frowned. 'As you requested, I have informed you of this development first.'

She swallowed hard. 'That was very—very thought-ful of you.'

'I have my moments.'

'Yes. Yes, you do.' She nodded. 'I— Do you also know how it was they managed to replace their dead daughter with me?'

He gave a pained wince. 'Beth—'

'Please, Raphael!'

He nodded as he obviously heard the strain in her voice. 'As you already know, Carla Lawrence was Argentinian by birth. Several of the Lawrences' neighbours still live in the village of Stopley, and clearly remember the tragic and sudden death of their baby daughter from meningitis—'

'Oh, God…!'

Raphael frowned at the unnatural pallor of her cheeks. 'The rest of this can wait until later—'

'No! No,' she repeated more calmly as she looked across at Raphael with pleading tear-wet eyes. 'I—I want to hear it all now. I need to know. Please, Raphael,' she added gruffly.

He drew in a sharp breath, wishing that he weren't the one having to tell Beth these things. That she wasn't going to remember, to associate him with having imparted this knowledge, and hate him for it ever afterwards.

He had become used to Beth's outspokenness, her feistiness, and her anger, but her aversion to being any-where near him was something else completely. 'Would you rather wait until Cesar and Grace arrive to learn all of the details?'

'Cesar and Grace are coming here?' She groaned her dismay.

'They will be.' Raphael nodded confirmation. 'Cesar instructed me to inform him the moment I received conclu-sive proof as to Elizabeth Lawrence's demise,' he amended gruffly; after all, until a few minutes ago Beth had believed she was Elizabeth Lawrence, and so to her talking of Elizabeth Lawrence's death was the equivalent of talking of her own death.

'But you really haven't told him yet?' Beth pushed.

'I have said not.'

'And if I asked you to delay doing so for another day or so?' she prompted evenly.

Raphael looked at her through narrowed lids. 'And why would I want to do that?'

She drew in a ragged breath, her gaze a deep and steady brown as she looked across at him. 'Because I asked you to.'

'That does not tell me why, Beth,' he murmured softly.

She breathed deeply. 'Because I want you to take me to the churchyard at the village of Stopley tomorrow, so that I can see Elizabeth's grave for myself, and place some flowers there in remembrance of her. I want— Raphael, I *need* to say goodbye to her, before I can even think of saying hello to Gabriela Navarro.'

'Beth—'

'This is important to me, Raphael!'

Yes, he could see by the glitter of tears in Beth's eyes, and the brave determination of her expression, that this was very important to her.

Important enough for Raphael to ignore Cesar's instructions and do as Beth asked?

CHAPTER EIGHT

'IT'S SUCH A little grave…' Beth murmured huskily as she straightened to stand beside Raphael in the peaceful silence of the churchyard, having just placed the small bouquet of yellow roses she had brought with her on top of the grave that bore the indisputable inscription on the headstone: 'Elizabeth Carla Lawrence, aged two years, beloved daughter of James and Carla Lawrence. Rest in Peace our Angel.'

Beautiful sentiments, but the small person in that grave certainly wasn't Beth, who for most of her life had believed *she* was Elizabeth Carla Lawrence.

The real Elizabeth Lawrence had lived the two brief years of her life in the small village of Stopley that Beth and Raphael had driven through just a few minutes ago on their way to the grey-stone church and its surrounding graveyard at the furthest end of the village. Beth was grateful that Raphael had opted to drive the two of them to Stopley himself in one of the less ostentatious Navarro vehicles. It was a village Beth had had no knowledge of until yesterday, let alone had ever lived in, as a young child or at any other time.

She had barely slept at all the previous night, insisting on going in to work this morning. She hadn't told Raphael why she had insisted, but she had spent part of the morning speaking to Graham Selkirk, her immediate boss, explaining the situation as much as she felt able to without involving the Navarro family, before requesting a month's leave of absence. Even if she hadn't confided the fact to Raphael yet, their visit to Stopley that afternoon was only the start of the process of her accepting, once and for all, that she really was Gabriela Navarro. Graham Selkirk would have been perfectly within his rights to deny Beth's request for leave, and so giving her no choice but to give immediate notice. Instead he had told her to take as long as she needed to sort out her family problem, and that her job would be waiting for her when she came back, if she still wanted it.

That last comment had given Beth the sneaking suspicion that Cesar's interference might have had something to do with Graham's easy acquiescence to her request. Cesar probably hadn't bought the company, yet, but no doubt he'd had a quiet word with whoever did own it! But she was too upset, too tense, from her sleepless night, and the thought of her planned visit to Stopley later that afternoon, and the ensuing consequences of that visit, to bother questioning Graham on the subject. What was the point, when all of the evidence now pointed to her being Gabriela Navarro? And Cesar had already made it more than clear that he did not approve of his sister Gabriela working in an English publishing house, that her place was in Argentina, with her family...

Raphael had no idea what answer to make in reply to Beth's husky comment. It was indeed a tiny grave. And six feet beneath that top layer of grass were the remains of two-year-old Elizabeth Carla Lawrence. The daughter of James and Carla Lawrence.

'You never did finish telling me how you think they managed all this.' Beth spoke again quietly. Raphael had

no doubts that she was referring to the Lawrences, and
that she was questioning how they had replaced their own
dead daughter with the child of another couple, Carlos and
Esther Navarro, who had mourned for their own child for
the past twenty-one years.

'We have managed to piece together the information
that the Lawrences visited Carla's family in Buenos Aires
a month after Elizabeth died.' He spoke evenly, dressed in
one of his dark and formal three-piece suits, a dark grey tie
knotted neatly at the throat of his white shirt. 'The same
month that Gabriela was taken. They travelled alone on
their way to Argentina, but when they flew back to England a month later their two-year-old daughter Elizabeth
accompanied them.'

Beth's eyes were like two dark bruises as she turned
to look up at him, appearing very pale and slender, even
ethereal, with her blond hair loose about her shoulders
and wearing a pair of fitted brown trousers with a brown
figure-hugging sweater. 'Is it really that easy to abduct
someone else's child?'

'No, it is not,' Raphael assured her softly. 'All we can
assume is that Elizabeth's name had not yet been removed
from her mother's passport. As you know, the Navarros
had not publicly announced that their daughter had been
abducted, for fear it might jeopardise her being returned
to them, and as such the airport authorities would have
had no reason to suspect that the golden-haired two-year-
old little girl with the Lawrences was not their own child.'

She nodded woodenly. 'But what about when they returned to Stopley? Surely someone must have noticed that
they had a little girl with them who closely resembled Elizabeth but couldn't possibly be her?'

'The Lawrences did not return to Stopley.' Raphael grimaced. 'The neighbours Rodney spoke to yesterday said

that James Lawrence returned only briefly, in order to pack
up the contents of their house. He told them that Carla did
not feel she could return to the home where they had lived
with Elizabeth, that they were moving to—'

'Kent,' Beth supplied softly.

'Yes,' Raphael confirmed huskily, knowing that was
the county in which Beth had supposedly spent the first
five years of her life.

'And so Elizabeth Lawrence lived and then died.'

'Yes.'

Beth drew in a long and steadying breath. 'Then I really
am Gabriela Navarro. Or Brela, as Cesar called his little
sister. Strange the two names, Brela and Beth, should be
so similar,' she added flatly.

'Yes.'

She looked up at Raphael quizzically. 'You seem to have
got stuck in a groove.'

In truth Raphael was full of admiration for the way in
which Beth was responding to learning, once and for all,
that she really wasn't Elizabeth Lawrence. That she never
had been. Apart from her pallor, and that bruised look to
her eyes, Beth—Brela—was remaining remarkably calm,
considering her whole life had just been turned on its head.

His first instinct was to take her into his arms, and
offer her the comfort she so desperately needed, but there
was a distance to her now, a barrier encircling her, that
didn't encourage anyone to so much as touch her, let alone
try to comfort her. 'Have you seen enough?' he prompted
abruptly instead.

She made no effort to walk away as she turned back to
look down at the gravestone. 'Do you think my—the Lawrences, ever came back here? To visit their real daughter's
grave, I mean?'

'Perhaps.' Raphael shrugged. 'There is no way of knowing one way or the other.'

Beth grimaced. 'I don't like to think of her—to imagine Elizabeth, being left here all alone, year after year—'

'Beth—'

'It's all right, Raphael.' She turned to give him a strained smile. 'You don't need to worry, I'm not going to break down in floods of tears. I haven't returned your silk handkerchief from last time yet!'

Raphael had no idea how to go about dealing with this calm and coolly collected—this unreachable—Beth. 'I have plenty of other handkerchiefs,' he assured her gruffly.

She gave a firm shake of her head. 'I'm not going to cry.'

'Then perhaps you should.'

'Why?' Her eyes flashed up at him darkly and her hands were clenched at her sides. 'Don't feel sorry for me, Raphael. I didn't even know the real Elizabeth Lawrence.'

'You are upset.'

'Of course I'm upset!' Beth confirmed fiercely. 'Wouldn't you be upset, if you had just visited your own graveside?'

Raphael drew in a hissing breath at the stark reality of that statement; Beth had, effectively, just done exactly that. The fact that she was dealing with this situation as calmly as she was, with a dignity far beyond her years, only increased his admiration for her; a dangerous admiration, considering his completely physical response to this particular woman.

'Yes.' He nodded. 'We should go, Beth.' He reached out to clasp her arm, with the intention of escorting her from the churchyard.

She flinched away from his touch. 'But I'm not Beth any more, am I? I'm Gabriela.'

Raphael looked down at her searchingly as his hand

dropped slowly back to his side, noting the flush that had now entered her cheeks, and the unnatural brightness to those beautiful dark eyes. 'I am sure that the Navarros will continue to call you Beth, if that is what you prefer.'

'I would *prefer* that none of this nightmare had ever happened,' she dismissed tautly. 'But that obviously isn't going to happen. And what would be the point of asking them to call me Beth, when she no longer exists?'

'Of course you exist—'

'No-I-don't.'

He flinched at the fierce evenness of her tone. 'You—'

'Time to go, Raphael.' She turned away abruptly, not waiting to see if he accompanied her as she walked swiftly through the graveyard to where they had left the car parked by the side of the road.

Raphael followed her slowly, for once in his life unsure as to what to do or say next…

The effort to hold back the tears burned the back of Beth's throat as she sat in the car beside Raphael while he drove them away from the village of Stopley—away from Elizabeth Lawrence's tiny grave.

She so wanted—needed—to cry. Wanted to scream and shout, too, as she shed those tears of pain and loss. The pain and loss she felt for the death of Elizabeth Lawrence, that two-year-old baby back there in the graveyard, as well as her own.

And if she felt this way after seeing Elizabeth Lawrence's grave, how much more deeply Esther and Carlos Navarro must have suffered after the disappearance of their own beloved daughter, never knowing what had become of her, or whether she was alive or dead. An uncertainty that had finally driven the couple into living apart, Esther returning to her native America, while Carlos remained in

Argentina, when they could no longer even look at each other without thinking of the baby daughter they had lost.

As for Cesar…Beth knew from Grace that he had lived all of his adult life with the guilt of his baby sister's disappearance hovering like a dark shadow over his heart. Gabriela had been taken from her pushchair in the park during the few minutes she had been left unattended while their nanny helped him untangle his kite from some bushes.

The biggest tragedy of all perhaps was that while Beth could sympathise with all of the Navarros' pain, she couldn't just step back in Gabriela's designer shoes and become the daughter they had lost. Any more than she could just turn on a switch and feel an outpouring of familial love for all of them. She might be Gabriela Navarro—she had no choice now but to accept that was who she really was—but she wasn't and doubted she ever could be the Gabriela Navarro her 'family' so longed for, and wanted her to be…

Maybe, with time, she might come to care for them all—although the arrogant Cesar was going to be something of a challenge!—but she very much doubted it was ever going to be enough, that *she* was ever going to become Gabriela enough to satisfy the hunger for the daughter, the sister, the Navarro family had suffered under for the past twenty-one years.

Grace's marriage to Cesar would help, of course, but only in as much as Grace would also become a part of the family to whom Beth really belonged. It wasn't going to help with Beth's own feelings of emotional detachment where the Navarro family were concerned. Esther and Carlos were nice people, and she liked them both a lot as Grace's future in-laws, but she felt nothing else for them. No sudden recognition of them being her real parents. Nor did she have any earth-shattering memories of the older brother she had reputedly adored and who had so obviously also adored her. It was—

'Would you care to stop somewhere for an early dinner?'

Beth turned to look blankly at Raphael for several seconds before his words managed to permeate the bleak fog of her own thoughts, a glance at her wristwatch showing it was almost seven o'clock in the evening. Meaning she must have stood at Elizabeth Lawrence's graveside for almost two hours. No wonder Raphael had suggested it was time for them to leave!

And she didn't really want to return to Cesar's Hampshire estate just yet, knowing that Raphael would then feel obliged to telephone the Navarro family and tell them about their visit to Stopley and Elizabeth Lawrence's grave.

Not that she was in the least hungry, either—in fact, Beth felt slightly sick!—but she was more than willing to pretend to eat an early dinner if it meant a delay in returning to Hampshire and Raphael's phone call to Cesar. A glass of wine, or two, would be more than welcome, too. 'Does that mean that Kevin Maddox still hasn't managed to employ a cook for the estate?' she attempted to tease.

'I have no idea,' Raphael dismissed tightly. 'I just thought that you might prefer it if we did not return there just yet.'

And, as usual, he had thought correctly. Strange how well Raphael had come to know her in such a short time.

'An early dinner sounds lovely, thank you,' she accepted huskily.

'I'll stop at the next suitable place I see.' Raphael nodded grimly, having been well aware of the tumult of thoughts that had been going through Beth's beautiful head since they left Stopley. Strained as his relationship was with his own father, Raphael had always known exactly who he was and what was expected of him, and couldn't even begin to relate to the confusion of emotions Beth must be feeling right now. Sadness at the death of the real two-year-old Elizabeth Lawrence, and the added trauma of having to accept what Beth had tried so hard to deny: that she really was the missing Gabriela Navarro, daughter of Esther and Carlos Navarro, and sister of Cesar Navarro.

Although she seemed to put that confusion firmly to the back of her mind as Raphael opened the car door for her a few minutes later outside the olde worlde country inn he had chosen to stop at. 'Nice.' She smiled her approval as she straightened beside him.

Raphael was more aware of Beth's disturbing presence beside him than he was the charm or otherwise of the country inn. Her hair smelt of the tartness of lemons, and although her face was still unnaturally pale it was also ethereally beautiful, and her slender and sensuous curves were shown to advantage in the brown fitted sweater and trousers.

She turned to look up at him when she received no reply to her comment, her breath catching in her throat as she obviously saw that awareness burning in Raphael's eyes as he found himself unable to look away from her. 'Would you please kiss me, Raphael?' she invited huskily as she took a step closer to him.

'Why?'

'Honestly?'

'Yes.'

Her eyes darkened. 'Because I want—*need* to know I exist, Raphael. To know that I'm still me!'

It was a plea that Raphael was unable to deny as he felt those soft and warm curves pressing against him, his gaze continuing to hold Beth's as his head slowly lowered and he captured those full and sensuous lips beneath his own, before his arms moved about her waist and he moulded those soft pliable curves against his much harder ones.

It had been his intention to kiss her gently, to offer her the comfort rather than passion, but those intentions evaporated at the first taste of Beth's lips, Raphael giving a low groan of his own need as the kiss deepened, his tongue sweeping into the heat of her mouth as the hardness of his arousal fitted snugly against the heated well between Beth's thighs—

'Maybe the two of you should get a room?' an indulgently teasing voice suggested lightly.

Raphael pulled back sharply to look down at Beth searchingly for several seconds before he turned to face the middle-aged man standing behind them. 'I apologise.' He bowed stiffly as he grasped Beth's arm and moved her slightly aside from where they were blocking the doorway.

'No problem,' the older man assured him dismissively. 'I might have been tempted to do the same with such a pretty young lady.'

He gave them a smiling nod before entering the inn.

'Well, that was…a little embarrassing,' Beth dismissed ruefully, her gaze avoiding meeting Raphael's as she turned and briskly followed the other man inside the intimacy of the inn.

Raphael followed more slowly, his mouth tightening as the older man, now standing at the bar ordering a drink, nodded to him in passing as the waitress took them to a table looking out onto the gardens.

He should not have given in to the temptation to kiss her. Certainly should not have placed her in a position of public ridicule.

Beth waited until the waitress had taken their food order and served the bottle of wine Raphael had ordered, before taking an obviously much-needed gulp of it. 'The notice outside said they have rooms available here, so maybe we should take that man's advice.' She looked across at him.

Raphael drew in a sharp breath, a frown having appeared between his eyes as he looked up from the menu he had been studying. 'I do not think so,' he finally bit out tautly as Beth finished off the rest of the wine in her glass.

'Why not?' she prompted as the waitress hurried over to refill her wine glass.

He arched dark brows. 'Well, for one thing, your brother is my best friend, and as such I know Cesar well enough to know that he would wish to inflict actual bodily harm on anyone who took advantage of you at this moment.'

'Even if my invitation means I'm the one intending to take advantage of you?'

'Even then,' he assured her harshly. 'Secondly, you appear to be well on your way to becoming inebriated, and I do not seduce inebriated women.'

'What if she's the one doing the seducing?'

'Beth—'

'Raphael?' she came back softly as she deliberately picked up the now full wine glass and took another challenging sip.

'Eat something before you drink any more, hmm?' He reached across the table and carefully removed the glass from her hand before placing it down onto the table between them.

She leant back in her chair. 'And if I promise to eat something, and not drink any more wine, are you still going to refuse me?'

He drew in a hissing breath. 'You are upset, and not thinking clearly at the moment—'

'I'm thinking clearly enough to remember I wasn't in the least inebriated when the two of us last made love.'

Raphael breathed deeply. 'That was different.'

'In what way was it different?' She arched one blond brow. 'Because that time you were the one to instigate the seduction rather than me?'

'No, of course not,' Raphael snapped his impatience. 'But you have received a shock today, and you are upset, and I should not have kissed you just now.'

'Raphael, if you don't make love to me tonight, then I'm going out to find someone else who will,' she assured her determinedly.

Raphael's eyes narrowed as he easily noted the reckless light in those dark brown eyes, and the rebellious tightening of her lips.

'Do you have someone in mind?'

Her chin rose challengingly. 'And if I do?'

'Then I would advise against it,' he bit out harshly.

'And if I choose not to take your advice?'

His shoulders moved in a stiff shrug. 'That is your prerogative, of course.'

'And you're saying it wouldn't bother you?'

Oh, yes, it would bother Raphael very much to imagine Beth making love with another man. More than he cared to think about. Or acknowledge.

She sat forward, her dark gaze holding his as she spoke softly. 'I could feel how much you wanted me a few minutes ago…'

How much Raphael still wanted her, his engorged shaft a throbbing ache between his thighs. 'You are playing with fire, little one,' he advised gruffly.

Beth already knew that, was only too aware of the desire she could still see burning in Raphael's piercing blue gaze. And she longed for that burn, wanted to be alone with Raphael, in the privacy of a bedroom, and know the full force of the desire he had minutes ago demonstrated he felt for her. And not, as Raphael seemed to think, because she was 'upset' or 'not thinking straight'. Oh, that probably played some part in it, was allowing her to do and say things she might otherwise not have said or done. But the truth of the matter was she wanted Raphael to make love to her. Had wanted that since the moment she first looked at him over a week ago...

She reached over and placed her hand on top of his as it rested on the table. 'I don't want anyone else but you, Raphael.'

He gave an impatient shake of his head. 'You don't even know me—'

'I know far more about you than you realise,' she assured him softly. 'For instance, I know that you're thirty-three years old, that you went to the same school as Cesar, that your father owns a successful vineyard and ranch in Argentina, but that for your own private reasons you are estranged from that father and prefer to work with Cesar, your closest friend, that your sister Rosa is special to you—'

'Enough!' A nerve pulsed in his tightly clenched jaw as he glared across the table at her.

Beth was prevented from answering him for several minutes as she removed her hand as the waitress arrived with their food, a cheese salad for her, and chicken and salad for Raphael. 'You're right, Raphael, I am upset at the moment,' she continued huskily once the two of them were alone again, 'and a little emotionally off balance from all that I've learnt today. But,' she continued firmly as he would have spoken, 'not so much that I don't know what I'm doing. What I'm asking.'

That nerve still pulsed in his tightly clenched jaw. 'And you want— Let me get this clear. You are asking that the two of us spend the night here together, making love?'

'Yes.'

He gave a shake of his head. 'It is a natural reaction to want to reaffirm life after the shock of death—'

'Elizabeth Lawrence died twenty-one years ago, Raphael.'

'As far as you are concerned, she died only hours ago!'

That was true. And Beth Blake had died hours ago as surely as Elizabeth Lawrence had. It now only remained for Gabriela Navarro to be reborn. But before that happened Beth wanted this one last thing for herself. Wanted to spend the night with Raphael, the man who had made it clear to her that he considered Gabriela Navarro to be off limits to him, for all of the reasons he had previously stated. 'Are you going to make me beg, Raphael?' she prompted huskily.

Raphael groaned inwardly. Dear God in heaven! The last thing he wanted was for Beth to beg him for anything, least of all to make love with her, something he had ached to do from the moment she had arrived in Argentina over a week ago.

He hadn't known exactly who she was at that time, of course, had only been introduced to her as Grace Blake's younger sister, but even so he had wanted her. Had taken one look at the beauty of her face surrounded by that cascade of raggedly styled blond hair, the lean and yet curvy lines of her body, and felt his shaft thicken with instant and pulsing arousal. The same desire and arousal that had consumed his every waking moment since.

So much so that having Cesar ask him to take care of Beth's security had been like asking a drug addict to watch over a heroine shipment, or the alcoholic to guard the distillery.

And now Beth was asking—offering to beg, if necessary—for him to make love to her...

CHAPTER NINE

USUALLY BETH HAD a problem knowing what the enigmatic Raphael was thinking or feeling at any given moment, but here and now, seated across a varnished dining table in an innocuous country inn, she had no problem at all reading the desire, battling with conscience, in the tightness of his expression. Right now, at this moment, Raphael wanted her as much as she wanted him, he just wanted her to be very sure as to why it was she was suggesting the two of them spend the night here together.

She breathed in deeply. 'Would you excuse me for a moment?' She placed her napkin carefully down on the table top before standing up.

'Beth?' Raphael reached out to lightly grasp her hand as she would have walked past him, his gaze searching as he looked up at her.

She gave him a reassuring smile. 'I'll only be a couple of minutes.'

'Oh.' His brow cleared and he slowly released her hand. 'I noticed the sign for the ladies' room out in the hallway as we came in.'

'So did I.' She nodded her thanks before walking away.

Except Beth wasn't going anywhere near the ladies' room...

* * *

Raphael was more than a little concerned when Beth hadn't returned within ten minutes of leaving the table; either she had become ill once she reached the privacy of the ladies' room or she had decided to somehow leave without telling him to go in search of that 'someone else' who would agree to spend the night with her. The former he could deal with, if it became necessary, but his discomfort at the thought of it being the latter wasn't helped in the least by the fact that the older man from earlier kept shooting him raised-eyebrow glances from the bar area—as if he also suspected that Beth might have run out on him!

Just when Raphael had reached the point where his security instincts told him he had to go in search of her, he sensed her presence beside him—and smelt that wonderful fresh feminine smell that was entirely Beth: lemons, flowers, and warm enticing woman! His breath caught in his throat, a quiver running the length of his spine, as she paused to run her fingers lightly over his shoulder and down his arm before moving forward to resume her seat across from him at the table.

'Sorry about that—it took longer than I thought.' Her face was slightly flushed, her eyes a bright glittering brown, as she carefully placed a key attached to a numbered wooden square down on the table between them.

Raphael's gaze was riveted on that key, and its implications. 'What have you done?' he breathed softly.

'Nothing yet,' she came back pertly. 'But once we've finished our meal I'm hoping that the two of us will go upstairs and finish what we started outside. Unless you would rather forgo the rest of our meal and go upstairs to our bedroom now?'

Raphael's lids rose as he looked across at her, the slightly uncertain expression in her eyes, and the anxious way in which she chewed on her bottom lip, both a complete contradiction of her breezily confident tone.

'That is what you were doing just now—arranging a room for the two of us to stay here overnight?'

'Yes…' That anxiety had darkened her eyes now. 'Unless you would really rather not?'

Unless Raphael would rather not…!

He had been displeased at the thought of Beth having become ill from the strain she had been under these past few hours, from seeing that damning gravestone, but even so he was sure that was a problem he could have coped with. But the mere thought of Beth having somehow left here to return to London, in order to go to that 'someone else she had in mind to make love with her tonight', had made Raphael feel as angry as it did physically ill. If any man was going to make love to Beth tonight, then it was going to be him!

'You know, Raphael, it isn't in the least flattering that you're taking so long to make up your mind.' There was a brittle tension beneath her cajoling tone.

Raphael gave a tight smile. 'I am merely trying to decide whether you would benefit from finishing your meal, or whether it would be better for us to go straight upstairs.'

'Oh.'

He almost widened his smile at her look of confusion. Almost. He was too tense with need for this woman to find any real humour in this situation. 'Perhaps you are now having second thoughts?'

Her chin rose. 'Not in the least,' she assured him firmly.

He nodded. 'In that case, I think you might benefit from the extra energy the food will give you.'

Her throat moved convulsively as she swallowed, her cheeks having flushed a deep pink. 'That sounds…interesting.'

Raphael eyed her ruefully. 'But not what you were expecting my answer to be?'

Beth had no idea what she had expected Raphael's reaction to be when she returned to the table and told him she had arranged for the two of them to stay here together tonight. She only knew that she wanted him, wanted those hours of being aware of nothing else, of thinking of nothing else but Raphael, of saying to hell with the rest of the world as they explored and pleasured each other. She wanted that more than she wanted her next breath!

She moistened her lips with the tip of her tongue. 'Could we go upstairs now? Right now?' she added urgently, her knuckles showing white as she gripped the edge of the table.

He gave an abrupt nod. 'If that is what you wish.'

She gave a tremulous smile. 'A little enthusiasm on your part would be welcome about now!'

Raphael looked at her blankly for several long seconds before he breathed out raggedly, a nerve pulsing in his clenched jaw as he leant forward over the table, his eyes a deep and piercing cerulean blue as he easily held Beth's gaze captive. 'Would my telling you that I have remained hard and aching for you since we kissed outside earlier count as "enthusiasm"?'

Her breath hitched in her throat. 'Oh, yes…'

'Also that I have been able to think of little else but kissing and suckling your beautiful and responsive breasts since I last touched you there?'

Her eyes widened as she thought of the last time—the only time—Raphael had touched her breasts so intimately. That evening in the gym. Two days ago…

'That I have been longing to touch you again, to stroke between your thighs, to pleasure you, slowly and then harder, until your muscles tighten and ripple in orgasm about the thrust of my fingers?'

Beth's face was fiery hot as she found herself unable to look away from the fierceness of Raphael's gaze, so aroused just listening to him describe making love to her she could barely breathe; her nipples felt full and aching, between her thighs moist as her channel became swollen in anticipation of that sweet penetration, that hard little nubbin already an aching throb.

'And afterwards I want to taste you there,' Raphael continued softly. 'Take my time kissing slowly down your body, until I can place my lips and tongue on you—'

'Perhaps we should go now?' Beth had heard enough, was already so aroused by the things Raphael was saying to her that she was in danger of reaching that climax just sitting here listening to him describe all the wonderful things he was going to do to her.

'And then I want to thrust my tongue inside you, again and again, squeezing your breasts and plucking your nipples as I make you come that way the second time—'

'Raphael…!' She was so wet and aching now she shifted uncomfortably on the seat as her trousers felt too tight and restrictive.

'The third time I want to—'

'The third time?' She gasped weakly, her eyes wide, her cheeks flushed, and her skin feeling damp, just from listening to the sensuous and mesmerising rumble of Raphael's voice as it moved over her like a caress.

He nodded. 'A woman may have as many orgasms as the man is experienced enough to give her.'

'And you're very experienced?'

His mouth quirked self-derisively. 'Oh, yes.'

'And the man?' she challenged.

'Me?' He shrugged those impossibly broad shoulders.

'After the first two times—the first will be fast and hard, because I have wanted you for too long for it to be any other way, and the second slow and intense, because I want to explore every single part of your body before I allow myself the pleasure of plunging between your thighs a second time—it will be for you to decide how many more times, and in what ways, you will make me hard and hot for you.'

It was as if Beth had opened a door, pressed a switch somewhere deep inside Raphael, releasing a man who was dark and primal. A man who it seemed had held back in their lovemaking so far—out of a desire not to shock or alarm her?—but was making it clear he no longer intended doing so. His next comment confirmed that was his intention.

'Think carefully, Beth,' he warned gruffly. 'Be absolutely sure, before we go up those stairs together, that you want all that I want, because I doubt, once we are alone and both naked, that I will be able to stop from indulging in every erotic fantasy I have ever had about you. And there have been many,' he acknowledged wryly.

Beth wasn't sure that she *knew,* let alone was familiar with, all of the things promised in the hard sensuality of Raphael's glittering blue gaze. But she shivered with the anticipation of wanting to know. Oh, yes, here and now, with this man, she wanted that—wanted Raphael!—so very much…

She stroked her tongue across the dryness of her lips, drawing her breath in sharply as Raphael's eyes took on an almost feral fierceness as his heated gaze followed that sweeping caress. 'I told you, Raphael, I want *you,* all of you, in whatever way you want me.' And if that included lovemaking as she had never imagined it, let alone come close to experiencing, in the one or two forays she had made into the physical side of a relationship during her years at university, then so be it.

'And I need to know it is not something you will regret in the morning!' he rasped harshly.

Beth winced. 'Can't we let the morning take care of itself?'

A nerve pulsed in his clenched jaw. 'No.'

She frowned, not sure what Raphael wanted from her—and knowing that most men of her acquaintance would take what she was offering, and to hell with the why she was offering!

But not Raphael...

Was she in love with him? Was that the real reason she wanted to spend her last night as Beth Blake in Raphael's arms?

She did know that Raphael affected her like no other man she had ever met, that he had done so since the moment she first looked at him, arousing her interest, her own sexual fantasies, at the same time as he annoyed her.

But Raphael was a physically experienced man in his thirties, not a boy as green as Beth was, and whatever he asked of her during the night ahead she knew she would gladly give. She didn't want to give herself—or Raphael!—the time to work out why that was. 'Could we not analyse the spontaneity out of this, Raphael?' she answered him impatiently.

'I just need you to be very sure—'

'I've said that I am!' Her eyes flashed darkly in warning.

He studied her intently for several long seconds before nodding abruptly. 'Very well. I have finished eating, if you have.' He ignored their half-eaten meals as he picked up the door key and stood up before moving round the table in preparation for pulling back Beth's chair for her.

Beth's heart was pounding so loudly in her chest, her hands shaking as she placed them on the table and rose determinedly to her feet, that she was sure Raphael must be able to hear, and see that trembling, as he waited for her to collect her bag. He took a light hold of her arm as he accompanied her out of the restaurant and through the bar area to the staircase leading up to the rooms above, Beth hoping he would attribute those things to arousal rather than the nervousness that now held her in its grip.

The nervousness was not of Raphael. Never of Raphael. Whatever dark and primal desires she might have released from beneath his usually coolly controlled façade, Beth knew that he would never hurt her. She knew instinctively that Raphael was a man who preferred—who enjoyed—giving pleasure to a woman rather than inflicting pain.

No, it was her own inexperience Beth felt nervous about, and as to whether or not she would be woman enough to sustain and keep the intensity of Raphael's desire for her burning through the long hours of the night that lay ahead…

Raphael could feel Beth's nervousness increasing as they began to ascend the staircase to the floor above, feeling the trembling of her stiffly tense body as his hand remained firmly about her arm, able to hear her shallowly drawn breaths, and see how those huge brown eyes dominated the pale delicacy of her face as she stared straight ahead rather than at him.

She might deny having any doubts about the night ahead, but her behaviour and appearance said otherwise.

Her nervousness continued as they paused in the hallway so that Raphael could unlock the door to their room. 'I asked the landlord to give us the best room he has.'

Raphael glanced at her. 'I believe a comfortable bed to be our only requirement...'

'And an adjoining bathroom,' she added tensely. 'Which the landlord assures me this room has.'

'Good,' he clipped as he straightened before slowly turning the handle on the door to push it open, standing slightly to one side in the narrow hallway as he waited for Beth to precede him into a small bedroom. There was a low and dark-beamed ceiling overhead, the room like so many other hotel rooms, with its pink and cream chintz curtains and matching bedcover on the four-poster bed, the wallpaper and carpet in the same warm cream, several uninspiring paintings adorning the walls.

'Would you like to use the bathroom first or shall I?'

Raphael looked across the room at Beth as she stood silhouetted in front of one of the two windows, the darkening night sky behind her making her hair appear more gold shades than ever, her face still ethereally pale, her fingers tortuously twisting the innocent shoulder strap of her bag the only other outward show of her inner nervousness. 'You may go first,' he replied smoothly. 'I have several calls to make before I may call my time my own this evening.'

A frown appeared on her creamy brow. 'Would one of those phone calls happen to be the one to Cesar?'

He quirked dark brows. 'And if it is?'

Her breath hitched. 'Is it a good idea for you to talk to Cesar now, in the knowledge that you intend to seduce his little sister immediately afterwards?'

Raphael's mouth tightened. 'I believe you stated earlier that it was your intention to seduce me?'

Yes, she had said that, hadn't she? Beth acknowledged with an inner wince. And she hadn't changed her mind about that. It was just that, now she was alone with Raphael in this small bedroom, with that four-poster bed only feet away, he seemed so—so physically immediate, his sheer masculinity seeming to suck all the air out of the room.

'You're going to tell Cesar about—about, the success, of our visit to Stopley today?' She gave a pained frown.

Raphael gave a slight inclination of his head. 'I have respected your wishes in regard to that so far, but I think it only fair that I now inform Cesar of what we have discovered today, yes.'

She breathed out deeply through her nose. 'And no doubt he'll then either turn up in London tomorrow, accompanied by Grace, or maybe just send the private jet over to pick us both up and take us back to Argentina?'

'No doubt. Is that going to be a problem?' Raphael looked at her searchingly.

No, it wasn't a problem; Beth was already resigned to the fact that she now had no choice but to return to Argentina and the Navarro family—it was the reason she had asked Graham Selkirk for a month's leave this morning, after all. Her visit to Elizabeth Lawrence's grave earlier had been more of a courtesy, a show of respect for the baby girl who had died so long ago, rather than the proof Beth had said she needed to confirm the Navarros' claim of her being their long-lost daughter. If Raphael said the grave existed, then Beth had no doubts that it did. Just as she had known the consequences, to her, regarding its existence.

She gave a jerky nod. 'Okay, you make your calls and I'll go and use the bathroom first.' She quickly crossed the room to enter the adjoining room, locking the door securely behind her before leaning weakly back against it, her breathing sounding ragged in the small confines of the black-and-white bathroom.

She had wanted this to happen, asked for it, and now wasn't the time for her to be having a panic attack, or have second thoughts, because Raphael was about to give her exactly what she had asked him for...

Raphael continued to stand in the middle of the fussy bedroom as he stared at that closed bathroom door, knowing, despite her determination earlier, that Beth was having second thoughts—maybe even third and fourth ones!—as to the wisdom of her actions.

He had been deliberately graphic when he'd spoken to Beth earlier, when he had described the many ways he wished to make love to her. Not that he hadn't meant every word he'd said, because he had, but when—if—he ever made love with Beth, then he wanted her to be very sure it was what she wanted too, and not something she would regret in the morning. Something she would surely do if her only reason for spending the night with him was to block out who she must become tomorrow.

The two of them making love together was an irrevocable step, from which there would be no turning back, and Beth might not exactly hate him in the morning, but she would most certainly be embarrassed and self-conscious enough to want to avoid his company in future.

A future that required she become Gabriela Navarro, the daughter of Esther and Carlos Navarro, and sister of Cesar Navarro...

CHAPTER TEN

THE ONLY ILLUMINATION in the bedroom was from the lamp on the small bedside table nearest the bathroom when Beth returned to the bedroom fifteen or twenty minutes later, wearing only a towel wrapped about her and secured between her bare breasts. They had no luggage with them, and the inn simply wasn't big enough to supply bathrobes for its no doubt infrequent guests.

Raphael lay sprawled on the other side of the bed, having removed his jacket and tie, and completely unfastened and untucked his shirt so that it left his chest bared, revealing that silky dark hair and flat nipples the colour of deep rose against his bronzed skin, the top button of his suit trousers also unfastened.

He was also, from the slight heaviness of his breathing and his closed lids, very soundly asleep!

Beth moved to the vacant side of the bed to stare down at him in disbelief, not sure if she felt relieved or insulted that Raphael had somehow managed to fall asleep after making his telephone calls. It certainly wasn't in the least flattering to have the man who had earlier so vividly described how he intended making love to her fall into what appeared to be a dead sleep in the few minutes she had left him while she took a shower.

Especially when Beth considered she had spent those same minutes thinking of the night of lovemaking ahead!

She gave a low and disgruntled humphing sound as she turned back the bedclothes, turning off the light and plunging the room into darkness before dropping the towel and crawling in naked with her back turned towards Raphael. Her feelings of insult turned to ones of irritation as she realised that having Raphael on top of the bedcovers totally restricted her from pulling those bedclothes up over the bareness of her shoulders.

Beth tossed and turned for several minutes trying to get comfortable, and all the time she did Raphael remained totally unmoving beside her, his breathing still deep and steady. She finally sat up slightly to shoot a scowling glance in Raphael's general direction as she punched her pillows into comfortable submission, a part of her secretly wishing it were *him* she was punching. How dared Raphael just fall asleep after all those things he had described wanting to do to her? It was beyond insulting, it was—

'What did that poor pillow ever do to you?'

Beth froze at the husky sound of Raphael's voice, realising her eyes must have adjusted to the gloom of the bedroom as she raised startled lids and easily saw the light glitter of his eyes reflected in the moonlight shining in through the windows.

She moistened her lips. 'I thought you were asleep.' Her voice sounded unnaturally loud in the stilled silence of the room.

'I was,' Raphael drawled as he turned on his side, bending his elbow and resting his cheek against the palm of his hand as he looked down at her. 'You woke me up when you started attacking that defenceless pillow.'

'I was imagining it was you!' she came back tartly.

Having decided that it might be prudent on his part to

pretend to be asleep when Beth returned from taking her shower, to give her the option of a woman's prerogative to change her mind, Raphael now found himself giving a rueful shake of his head at Beth's obvious disgruntlement that he hadn't been waiting in impatient anticipation for her return. 'Why?' he prompted huskily.

Her eyes glittered at him in the semi-darkness. 'Why do you think?'

Raphael reached out and gently touched the soft creaminess of her heated cheek with his fingertips, feeling rather than seeing the quiver that shook her body at just that light caress. 'Would you believe me if I told you I was doing the gentlemanly thing and giving you the opportunity to change your mind?'

'Why?' she now returned softly.

He drew in a sharp breath. 'Because, despite the outrageous things I may have said to you in the restaurant downstairs, I *am* a gentleman.'

'Does that mean you weren't serious about those outrageous things?' There was a teasing lilt to her voice, her hair a silver-gold cascade over her bared shoulders in the moonlight.

'I meant every single word I said to you earlier,' Raphael assured her decisively. 'It is because I meant them, because I want you in all the ways I described, but saw and recognised your uncertainty once we reached this bedroom, that I decided it might be better if I were to go to sleep.'

'To give the appearance of being asleep?'

'Yes.'

All of Beth's earlier nervousness evaporated as she reached out to run her hands slowly up Raphael's chest and over the warmth of his shoulders as she scooted across the bed, only to give a groan of frustration as she realised the bedclothes continued to act as a barrier between them.

'Either you're going to have to get beneath the bedcovers or I'm going to get out from beneath them!' she muttered dryly.

'I believe it best that I be the one to join you,' he murmured ruefully as he drew her arms gently from about his neck before throwing back the bedclothes and standing up.

Beth's breath hitched in her throat as she lay back against the pillows and watched Raphael shed his shirt completely, the moonlight turning his bared and muscled flesh a deep and burnished gold, his shoulders impossibly wide, and his tapered chest and abdomen perfectly toned.

She stopped breathing altogether as he unzipped his trousers before pushing them, and his boxers, down the long length of his legs, before straightening.

He stood proudly naked, his body bathed in moonlight, his erection jutting up so long it reached his navel, and so thick around Beth doubted her fingers would be able to encircle it, the bulbous top appearing a dark and glistening purple.

She licked her lips with the tip of her tongue as she gazed unabashedly at that evidence of Raphael's arousal. 'You're beautiful,' she breathed softly.

Some of Raphael's tension eased at Beth's typical candidness.

'I believe that is supposed to be my line?' But not one he could have said when Beth presently held the bedclothes up to her chin in a death grip. 'Will you release the covers, Beth, and allow me to look at you, too?' he requested gruffly.

Her breasts barely moved beneath those bedcovers as she breathed shallowly, before she allowed her fingers to first slowly release those bedcovers, then push them down to her waist. She kicked them fully down the length of her body until she at last lay back naked and beautiful in the moonlight, her hair a shimmering silver-gold halo behind her on the pillows.

Raphael drew in a hissing breath as he hungrily drank in the sight of the ivory beauty of Beth's naked body: full and uptilting breasts tipped by strawberry-ripe nipples, her waist slender, hips flaring curvaceously, her legs long and shapely above slender and elegant feet.

His throat moved convulsively as he swallowed before speaking. 'Exquisite,' he groaned achingly.

Beth hadn't needed Raphael's verbal expression of his approval, had seen his response to her nakedness in the thickening, lengthening bob of his shaft and the intensity of the glistening juices at that purple tip.

Her nervousness became a thing of the past as she held out her arms to him. 'Come and make love with me, Raphael…'

His teeth gleamed whitely as he gave a predatory grin. 'First I intend making love *to* you,' he murmured throatily as he knelt on the bottom of the bed, gently pushing her legs apart before moving slowly upwards until he knelt between her thighs, the muscled firmness of his own hair-covered thighs pressing against her bared flesh, and sending quivers of awareness to her core, causing her inner folds to moisten and plump.

She watched beneath lowered lashes as Raphael bent his head and placed a brief but warm kiss against those golden curls, knowing he must be able to smell her salty-sweet arousal as the dark stubble on his chin rasped gently against her sensitivity, and causing a warm gush between her thighs.

Beth sucked in a breath, her head pushing back into the pillows, her back arching, as Raphael now touched her with just the warmth of his lips as they travelled butterfly soft across the flatness of her stomach before his tongue dipped into the well of her navel, gently probing, leaving a trail of moisture there, his hands lightly clasping her hips as his lips travelled higher still.

Beth's fingers clenched tightly into the sheet beneath her as she felt those butterfly kisses against her ribcage, just beneath but not quite touching the swell of her breasts, her nipples tingling, swelling like ripe fruit, in anticipation of the moment when those lips captured and suckled on those swollen berries.

It became exquisite torture as Raphael's lips now moved in an open-mouthed caress across and over her breasts, never quite touching those engorged nipples as his grip on her hips kept her from moving, shifting restlessly, as she felt the burn of desire between her thighs.

'Please, Raphael...!' She groaned her need longingly even as she arched her back, pushing her breasts up temptingly.

'Patience is most definitely a virtue when it comes to lovemaking, Beth,' he assured her softly, the warmth of his breath a tormenting caress against the curve of her breast.

She gave a pained moan. 'I ache, Raphael...!'

He stilled above her. 'Tell me where.'

'Everywhere! Oh, God, everywhere! My breasts, Raphael,' she added breathily as he remained still and silent.

'Cup your hands beneath them and offer them to me,' he encouraged throatily.

Beth didn't hesitate, her breath leaving her in a satisfied sigh as his open lips closed over one turgid peak and he suckled deeply, her hands moving up so that she could entangle her fingers in Raphael's hair as he continued to draw strongly on her nipple even as his tongue lathed a hot caress against that aching flesh, her sigh becoming a pleasurable gasp as Raphael lowered the lean length of his body gently down on top of her, the length of his hot and burning shaft further torment as it pressed against the moistness of her swollen folds.

It took all of Raphael's self-control not to hurry their lovemaking as he feasted on Beth's delicious breasts, her nipples as sweet as ripe strawberries against his tongue and the soft rasp of his teeth as one of his hands moved smoothly, caressingly, down over the silky flatness of her abdomen and stomach, before slowly moving lower, seeking out the swollen place between her thighs as she arched up into that caressing hand.

The tight bunch of flesh thrust engorged and swollen from beneath its protective hood in evidence of Beth's deep arousal, a low and keening cry escaping her lips as she began to climax as Raphael first stroked and then lightly squeezed her there, quickly thrusting a finger deep into her hot and clenching channel as he felt the climax rippling through her, prolonging her pleasure as his finger curved and stroked against the sensitive muscle deep inside her.

'Oh, God, oh, God, oh, God…!' Beth groaned and quivered and shook, her fingers digging painfully into Raphael's tensely muscled shoulders. His breathing was ragged as he kept her poised on the shuddering plateau of her release, holding her there with the press of his finger against something deep inside her as wave after wave after wave of undulating pleasure continued to rage and roil through her body. 'I can't take any more, Raphael…!' She gasped, her eyes wide as her hips strained and surged up again and again into that momentous release.

'You can,' he assured her fiercely as a second finger surged in hotly to join the first, the soft pad of his thumb caressing the overstimulated nubbin above, around and around, over and over again, until Beth thought she would explode into a million pieces that might never be put back together again.

'No, I—' Beth cried out as Raphael turned the attention of his lips, teeth and tongue to her other breast, at the same time as he released his hold on that pleasurable spot deep inside her, his fingers continuing to graze against that sweet spot with every thrust, Beth's pleasure riding higher still before she crashed, hurtled over the top in full and shuddering release.

Raphael held Beth in his arms, a worried frown marring his brow as the aftermath of her release continued to cause her to shake and quiver long after her body had attained its ultimate release, the wetness of the tears she had cried at the pinnacle of her climax still damp on her cheeks.

Had he been too rough with her? Taken her too far too fast? Raphael hadn't meant to frighten or alarm her; he had just gone past the point of being able to stop himself from accepting everything she so freely offered, and in return giving her everything back as he did all that he could to return the pleasure her uninhibited responses were giving him.

But the continued trembling of her body as she lay curled against him, her hand resting limply across his chest, was unexpected—

'It's my turn now, I believe,' she purred throatily as she moved out of his arms and up onto her knees beside him before reaching out to curve her fingers about his hot and throbbing shaft.

Raphael drew in a sharp breath. 'Beth—'

'Shh.' She lay one silencing fingertip against his lips as she moved down the bed before moving to kneel between his parted thighs. 'You're so beautiful here, Raphael,' she murmured appreciatively, her breath a soft and torturous caress against the heat of the bulbously swollen top of his shaft.

Raphael groaned as he felt the hot lap of her tongue against his burning flesh.

'You taste delicious, too.' Her tongue now lapped greedily over that bulbous top, before probing gently into the slitted tip and then over and around the lip, until she found and lingered over the sensitive skin just beneath.

It was Raphael's turn to tense his fingers into the sheet beneath him as he fought to maintain control as Beth raised her head before lowering her lips over him, at the same time as her fingers began to lightly pump his long and throbbing length, and her other hand cupped beneath the tautness of his sac.

She made a low and satisfied humming noise in her throat as she found a rhythm to her caresses, Raphael groaning his pleasure each time she took him to the back of her throat, that humming sending electrified jolts of pleasure down the length of Raphael's shaft as he felt the churning, boiling for release deep inside him. He reached down and placed his hands either side of her face to hold her exactly where she was as he gave himself up to the mindless need to thrust deep and hard into that hot delicious cavern.

He was poised, in danger of falling over the brink of that release, until he finally found the strength to lift Beth's head up and away from him, groaning as he instantly felt the warmth of her breath as a hot caress against his moist and still straining shaft.

'I have changed my mind, I badly want to be inside you when you come a second time,' he quickly explained as she looked down at him with hurt and questioning brown eyes. 'And I need to get protection before I do that,' he added regretfully, hating even the thought of that necessary layer of latex between himself and Beth.

'Protection,' Beth repeated blankly, feeling slightly dazed and more than a little bereft as Raphael moved to sit on the side of the bed, shoulders wide, his back long and muscled as he leant forward to pick up his trousers.

'Unless…' He glanced back at her over one of those shoulders. 'I am clean if you are?'

Beth blinked. 'I just took a shower…'

'That is not the sort of clean I meant,' Raphael cajoled lightly as he turned fully to face her. 'Oral contraception is not considered enough nowadays, Beth.'

Contraception! Dear Lord, when Raphael had said just now that he was 'clean' he meant—he meant—

How naïve could she get? How bloody naïve and—and stupid of her not to have realised Raphael was referring to *healthily* clean, as in having a doctor's certified assurance that he was free of sexual disease.

And how much of a mood killer was that!

Beth hadn't expected hearts and flowers from this man—that certainly would have been naïve of her with a man of Raphael's age and experience!—but she hadn't expected him to break off in the middle of the heat of their lovemaking to question her previous sexual habits, either!

It might be necessary nowadays, but it was also damned humiliating. And embarrassing.

She sat back on her heels as she drew in a deep and ragged breath. 'I'm clean, too, Raphael,' she assured him dully.

He nodded. 'You also have been checked in the last three months?'

'I—' Beth paused, chewing on her bottom lip for several seconds before answering him. Her own mood had certainly been ruined by this conversation, and she had a feeling that what she was about to say was going to kill all Raphael's desire, too… 'I've never been checked, Raphael. Because there's never been a need for me to do so.' Her chin rose as if in challenge.

It was Raphael's turn to look at her blankly now, a frown appearing between his eyes as he watched Beth stand before picking up the towel she had discarded earlier, to once again wrap it firmly about her nakedness before fastening it tightly between her breasts.

'I do not—' That frown was erased as Raphael's eyes widened incredulously. 'Are you trying to tell me you are still a virgin?'

Her eyes flashed darkly. 'I'm not "trying" to tell you anything, Raphael. I *am* telling you I'm still a virgin!'

'A virgin,' he repeated flatly, his incredulous gaze remaining fixed on her as he ran a hand agitatedly through the shortness of his thick dark hair.

Beth gave an annoyed frown at his reaction. 'It's unfashionable, I know,' she drawled irritably. 'But it isn't exactly the contagious disease your tone seems to imply it is!' He couldn't have sounded more horrified if she had told him she had the plague!

Raphael stood up abruptly, totally unconcerned with his own nakedness as he moved around the bed to stand just feet away from her. Although Beth couldn't help noticing that the fierceness of his erection had deflated somewhat, that beautiful shaft jutting out at half-mast rather than erectly flush with his navel.

'You are a virgin,' he repeated carefully.

'Yes.' Beth knew she sounded defensive, but she just couldn't help it; Raphael was behaving as if she were a lumbering dinosaur in a world of elegant gazelles!

He gave a slow shake of his head. 'And yet you were going to—minutes ago you were about to let me—' His mouth firmed, his jaw tightening as his hands clenched into fists at his sides. 'Beth, has no one told you that your virginity is a precious thing, and not to be given lightly?'

Lightly? Raphael believed—he thought she had made love with him out of curiosity, like some sort of childish flexing of her sexual powers?

She might have tried to avoid analysing her feelings for this man earlier, but that didn't mean she hadn't innately known what those feelings were. That somewhere, somehow, in amongst the hours they had spent arguing or annoying each other, and the hours she had spent denying she was Gabriela Navarro, she had managed to fall in love with him. Deeply, wildly, irrevocably in love. With Raphael Cardoba.

No doubt something else Raphael didn't want to hear...

What a fool she was. What an absolute idiot, not to have realised before tonight what was happening to her. Not that she could have prevented herself from falling for Raphael; she knew falling in love wasn't like that. She doubted her sister, Grace, would have fallen in love with a man as complicated as Cesar if it were! And now Beth had fallen in love with a man who was just as complicated. A man older and far more experienced than her. A man who seemed to have as many issues with his family as she had.

A man who had earlier made no secret of the fact that his interest in her was purely sexual...

Had been purely sexual.

Because Beth had no doubts that her admission of physical innocence had managed to kill even that.

'—drive back there now—Beth, are you even listening to me?' Raphael prompted hardly as he realised her attention had wandered elsewhere.

Although how she had managed to do that he had no idea, his own thoughts solely on the fact that he had almost taken her innocence tonight. He had thought that Beth, although perhaps not as experienced as he was, had at least been to bed with a man before tonight. The shock of realising she hadn't, and that he had almost taken her innocence without thought or due consideration, would haunt him for a very long time.

As it was, he was furious. Not with Beth. But with himself. How could he have been so stupid not to have realised, not to have known, that she had never taken a lover before tonight?

Yes, Beth had an answer for everything. And yes, she gave every appearance of being a modern young woman with a definite mind of her own. And she had also been the one to inform him earlier that he either took up the offer to become her lover tonight or she would find another man who would. But even then, *even then,* she hadn't given any indication that she had taken any previous lovers.

The question as to why she had chosen him to be her first lover was the least of Raphael's concerns at this moment. Getting Beth home—at least, back to Cesar's estate in Hampshire—and far away from any breath of scandal being attached to her name, because of the time she had spent here with him tonight, was Raphael's main priority. Everything else could be discussed at a later date.

Or not, if the challenging tilt to Beth's chin was any indication...

'Get dressed,' Raphael instructed harshly as he bent to collect up his own clothes.

She focused on him with effort. 'Dressed?'

He nodded abruptly. 'We are only about an hour away from the estate, and in the circumstances it would be best if we returned there tonight, after all.'

Best for whom? Beth wondered heavily as Raphael turned his back on her to begin pulling on his own clothes, and leaving her with no choice but to go back into the adjoining bathroom, where her clothes were, and lock the door before redressing.

Not that she thought there was any chance of Raphael entering the bathroom uninvited; he had made it more than clear that he had no intention of remaining in this hotel bedroom with her for another minute longer than he needed to!

Raphael didn't speak to her when she came back into the bedroom a few minutes later to find him once again dressed in his three-piece suit, white shirt and meticulously knotted tie—and looking absolutely nothing like the sensual and predatory man who had made love to her such a short time ago. And whom she had made love to.

Instead he looked grimly remote as he opened the bedroom door for her to precede him out of the room and down the stairs, handing her the keys to the car so that she could continue outside as he disappeared to settle the bill with the landlord.

Any dignity Beth might have managed to salvage, after Raphael's rejection of her when he realised her physical innocence, completely evaporated at the realisation she had just spent two hours in a hotel bedroom with a man before checking out again.

Oh, God…

CHAPTER ELEVEN

BETH'S TOTAL MISERY continued during their silent breakfast together the following morning, after a restless and sleepless night on her part. Although Raphael, apart from that brooding silence, behaved and appeared as coolly distant as ever, his expression harsh, despite his casual appearance in a pair of black denims and blue shirt.

Not that either of them ate any breakfast, the aching pain in the pit of Beth's stomach robbing her of any appetite for food, and Raphael seeming equally uninterested as the two of them just drank several cups of coffee together in that total silence.

Raphael finally spoke as they cleared away at the end of the meal. 'Cesar sent the jet for us overnight, and it is now refuelling and waiting at the private airport in preparation for flying us back to Argentina today.'

That Raphael couldn't wait to get back to Buenos Aires, before no doubt discharging all responsibility for her, was more than obvious from his frostily aloof manner and the arctic chill of his gaze as he looked down his arrogant nose at her.

Beth gave a tight smile as she straightened from loading the dishwasher, ironically wearing similar clothes to Raphael: black denims and a green cotton shirt. 'I guess those alterations to my house weren't necessary, after all!'

Raphael's eyes narrowed. 'They will be very necessary when you decide to return to England.'

'And when do you think that will be?' she came back dryly. 'If Cesar has his way, his little sister will never be allowed to leave Argentina ever again!'

Raphael scowled darkly. 'I had thought you had more self-determination than to allow Cesar to dictate your movements in future.'

Beth rounded on him fiercely, her eyes flashing darkly and her hands clenched into fists at her sides.

'How dare you talk to me like that? I haven't finished yet,' she added warningly as Raphael would have spoken. 'How do you have the nerve to stand there, talking down to me because I've decided to at least try to be Esther and Carlos's daughter, when your relationship with your own father is so obviously non-existent?'

Beth had spent quite a lot of the previous night sitting in a bedroom chair staring out of the window as she thought about her future as Gabriela Navarro—when she wasn't thinking about Raphael and reliving the humiliation of his rejection of her, and his terse goodnight to her once they were back at the estate, that was! For all her words of rebellion before she and Raphael left Argentina, Beth simply couldn't see the Navarro family happily letting her trot off back to England, and her house and job here, once Grace and Cesar were married.

Quite what she was supposed to do as Gabriela Navarro, Beth had no idea, never having had any dealings with heiresses, Argentinian or otherwise. But she had a feeling that it would involve hours and hours of shopping for suitable clothes, so that she could be taken out to suitable parties and dinner parties, and be introduced to suitable people. People as rich and privileged as the Navarro family.

All of which sounded like total misery to Beth.

At the same time as she knew she owed it to Esther and Carlos, her real parents, to at least try to fit into their world. To try to become their daughter again. Even if it was the last thing she felt like doing.

The *first* thing she felt like doing was getting as far away from Raphael Cordoba, and those humiliating memories of last night, as she possibly could!

And instead she was now going to spend hours and hours on a plane with him, suffering in silence while he continued to ignore her...

'I was not talking down to you—'

'It certainly sounded like it to me,' she came back determinedly. 'And from the little I know about your own situation, you appear to have walked out on your own family years ago, and never looked back!'

'That is not true.' A nerve pulsed in Raphael's tightly clenched jaw. 'I see all of my sisters whenever my other responsibilities allow.'

'Which doesn't appear to be very often,' Beth scorned. 'And you don't see your father at all. Why is that, Raphael?'

Raphael was beginning to wish he hadn't told Beth anything about his family. Most especially of the strained relationship that now existed between himself and his father.

'Or is it your stepmother you're avoiding?' Beth prompted astutely. 'Maybe because you begrudge your father the happiness of a second marriage?'

'My father's second marriage ended some years ago,' Raphael bit out tautly. 'And the only thing I begrudged was having his young wife make sexual advances to me—' Raphael broke off abruptly as he realised his anger had made him say far too much. Reveal far too much. 'It is time I—'

'Your stepmother made sexual advances to you?' Beth repeated incredulously.

Raphael easily read the all-too-familiar tenacity of Beth's expression. 'Yes,' he hissed.

'She tried to seduce you? Even though she was married to your father?'

'I think "seduce" is too polite a word for what Margarita intended in regard to her stepson, from the age of sixteen to nineteen, every time he returned for the school holidays,' he drawled scathingly.

'You were only sixteen when she first tried to seduce you?' Beth's eyes were wide. 'Why didn't you tell your father what was happening? Explain the situation to him and—'

'And what, Beth?' Raphael moved away impatiently. 'Expect that he would believe my word for what had happened over the word of the young and beautiful wife with whom he was totally besotted?' He eyed her mockingly.

'Your father knew about her—her sexual interest in you?'

'He eventually knew Margarita's version of things, yes,' Raphael bit out flatly.

'How?'

'You really do not want to know—'

'Yes. Yes, I really do, Raphael.' Beth nodded determinedly.

He sighed his impatience with her stubbornness. 'Remember that you were the one who asked me to tell you this,' he warned harshly as he drew in a deep breath before speaking again. 'I was out in the stables one day and she came into the stall where I was working, unbuttoning her blouse as she did so, revealing that she wore nothing beneath. I told her—as I had told her so many times before—that I was not interested in her in that way. She left her blouse partway unbuttoned and came towards me, her intentions obvious in her gaze and the lascivious expression on her face.' Raphael's own expression was bleak as he remembered the day that had changed his life for ever. 'I was too busy trying to fend off her attentions to realise that someone else had entered the stables, but apparently Margarita was not. To my surprise she suddenly pulled away from me and began screaming as she started pulling and tearing her blouse. By the time my father had hurried to the stall where we both were, Margarita had mussed her hair into a tangled mess and ripped several buttons from her blouse, the material itself gaping open to reveal her bared breasts.'

'Giving your father the impression that you had attacked her...'

'Yes.'

'But didn't you explain to him that you were completely innocent, that Margarita had done this to herself? That this wasn't the first time she had tried to proposition you?'

'How truly naïve you are, Beth.' Raphael eyed her pityingly. 'Of course I told him those things. But what should he believe, the evidence of his own eyes—Margarita's dishevelled appearance, her tears and distress, her accusations that I had tried to rape her—or the son who stood before him with a raging erection and denying any attraction for his young and beautiful stepmother? I was nineteen years old, Beth,' he added hardly as her eyes now widened in shock. 'An age when a woman's bared shoulder could give me an erection, let alone a pair of magnificent breasts!'

Beth's cheeks felt hot with embarrassment at Raphael's last comment. Shocked by the other things he had told her, but definitely embarrassed at hearing he had been aroused by his stepmother's advances, in spite of himself. 'Did your father throw you out?'

'Of course,' Raphael grated harshly. 'And I was only

too happy to go, believe me. But not before I had made
arrangements for Rosa to live with my sister Delores. My
sister was the only reason I had returned to the ranch for
as long as I had after my father's second marriage. Because
of Rosa's slowness Margarita took delight in being cruel
to her at times when my father was not looking.'

'She sounds an absolute bitch!' Beth muttered disgustedly.

'Yes,' he confirmed heavily. 'Have you heard enough
now?' he rasped scathingly. 'Can we now both get on with
our preparations to leave England today?'

'Not yet.' Beth gave a distracted shake of her head.
'Okay, I accept that at nineteen you probably weren't mature enough to deal with someone as vicious and manipu-
lative as your stepmother so obviously was, but what about
the last fourteen years? Have you been back, explained the
situation to your father?'

He eyed her impatiently. 'As it happens, I did not need
to do so.'

'Oh?'

Raphael grimaced. 'My father was less inclined to believe Margarita when, several years later, she tried to use
the same excuse after he found her naked, in their marriage bed, in the arms of one of his gauchos.'

'So you and your father are reconciled?'

A nerve pulsed in the tightness of his jaw. 'No.'

A frown appeared between her eyes. 'Why not?'

'Because we are Cordobas,' Raphael snapped.

Her expression grew rueful. 'Meaning that your father
is just as arrogant and proud as you are?'

'We are Cordobas,' he repeated, his eyes having turned
an icy blue.

'I've never heard anything so ridiculous in my life before!' Beth eyed him impatiently.

'That is because everything is so very black-and-white to you,' Raphael drawled derisively.

Beth felt slightly stung by his 'black-and-white' comment coming so soon after his accusation of her naiveté. And maybe she was both of those things, but it still hurt to have Raphael say it so cuttingly. 'This situation is black-and-white,' she insisted. 'Your father made a mistake fourteen years ago, a mistake you're both too proud to admit, and reconcile your differences. How old is your father, Raphael?' He frowned.

'What does that have to do with anything?'

'A lot, if you ever intend to heal the rift between the two of you.' Beth grimaced.

'And why would I wish to do that?'

'Because he's your father. Because he made a mistake, a mistake he's paid for dearly, first by losing his only son, and then the woman who had betrayed him. Because,' she continued firmly as Raphael would have spoken, 'in spite of everything, you love him…'

He drew himself up stiffly. 'This is none of your concern—'

'Of course it isn't,' Beth accepted impatiently. 'Except—'

'Can you be ready to leave in one hour's time?' Raphael rasped harshly.

'End of conversation?' she guessed ruefully.

Raphael nodded abruptly. 'End of conversation.'

Beth studied him closely for several seconds, knowing by his closed expression that he had no intention of discussing this subject any more with her today. If ever.

She nodded wearily. 'My bags are already packed and waiting upstairs.' She had been up before dawn—after sleeping fitfully for only a couple of hours—to pack her things in readiness for what she knew was their imminent departure to Argentina.

'We leave in one hour,' Raphael repeated harshly before striding forcefully out of the kitchen.

Beth's shoulders slumped the moment she was alone, tears scalding the backs of her eyes, and she reached out to grasp the edge of the kitchen table as her knees threatened to buckle beneath her, her conversation with Raphael, and the strain that existed between them now, having taken an emotional toll on her she was simply too tired to cope with.

Despite those shocking revelations in their conversation just now, Raphael had, to all intents and purposes, become a stranger to her these past twelve hours. He was no longer that mocking man she had known in Argentina, or the diligent bodyguard whose presence had annoyed and yet comforted her, both in Argentina and since they'd come to England. And he certainly wasn't the sensual lover of the night before, the man who had driven her insane with pleasure. Instead he was a man who now made it clear, with every word he spoke, that he wanted nothing more to do with her on a personal level.

And the pain of that realisation was worse than the sick feeling in the pit of her stomach—

'Sorry, Miss Navarro, I thought Raphael was in here?'

Beth turned slowly to find that Rodney had let himself into the house by the kitchen door without her even being aware of it. Because she was so lost in her own misery. The misery of being in love with a man who made it more than clear that he didn't want to be with her.

She straightened determinedly as she gave the security guard a forced smile. 'I think he went to Cesar's study.'

'That's fine.' The burly man nodded. 'Perhaps you can tell me what time we're leaving for the airport.'

Beth stilled. 'What time *we're* leaving for the airport?'

Rodney gave her a reassuring smile. 'I'm taking over as head of your security detail as from today.'

Beth felt all the colour drain from her cheeks. 'You are?' She knew she sounded like a parrot, and a slightly ridiculous one at that, but she was too stunned by what Rodney had just said to be able to pretend otherwise.

Rodney nodded happily, obviously completely unaware of Beth's distress at his disclosure. 'Raphael and I arranged it with Cesar last night.'

Last night? During Raphael's telephone conversation with Cesar at the inn, or after the humiliation Beth had suffered at Raphael's obvious rush to get them out of there once he had discovered she was still a virgin and, as such, untouchable?

Did it really matter *when* Raphael had arranged for Rodney to take over her security? The fact that he had done so spoke volumes; Raphael was no longer willing to even continue acting as her bodyguard.

She gave Rodney a tight smile. 'That's nice. Have you been to Argentina before?'

'No, but I'm really looking forward to it.' He grinned. 'Why don't we sit down and have a coffee together while we wait for Raphael to—to finish whatever it is he's doing, and I can tell you the little I know about it?' Beth suggested with a lightness she was far from feeling.

'That sounds great!' Rodney pulled out a chair and sat down at the kitchen table while Beth busied herself pouring them both a coffee before sitting down opposite him and commencing to tell him some of the sights she had seen on her last visit to Argentina.

Which was precisely where Raphael found the two of them when he entered the kitchen forty minutes later.

He came to a halt in the kitchen doorway as he heard

Beth laughing at something Rodney had just said to her. A relaxed and companionable laugh, so unlike the tension that had existed between himself and Beth since the previous evening.

Raphael still felt slightly numbed by how close he had come to taking Beth's precious virginity. And he was disgusted with himself for the intensity, the raw carnality, of his lovemaking. Not only was Beth an innocent, but Raphael had since realised, as his thoughts had gone over and over the sequence of their lovemaking last night, Beth wasn't just still a virgin but completely physically inexperienced.

Oh, no doubt she had shared a few passionate kisses with young men of her own age in the past, maybe even a little light petting, but nothing along the scale of Raphael's depth of lovemaking; in those circumstances, he was lucky she hadn't run screaming from the inn in total terror of his sexual demands!

He also, despite his denials, felt decidedly uncomfortable about their conversation earlier, in regard to his lack of decisive action regarding the rift between himself and his father. Perhaps it was time, after all, that he did as Beth had suggested and buried his pride before visiting his father?

Although the stricken look that came over Beth's face as she glanced up and saw him standing in the doorway didn't encourage Raphael into thinking of sharing that decision with her.

Any more than Raphael would wish for her to be aware of the feelings of jealousy that had ripped through him at the sight of her laughing so naturally with the man he had chosen to take his place as her personal bodyguard.

Cesar had been far from happy with his decision when the two men had spoken on the subject on the telephone the night before, but the uncharacteristic jealousy Raphael was feeling now, because he had only found Beth laughing and talking with another man—a man moreover who was also only a Navarro employee—only confirmed that Raphael had made the right decision in stepping down. He could not protect Beth, in the way she needed to be protected, when he only had to look at her to have his head flooded with memories of their lovemaking, and to burn with an inner desire to make love to her again.

No, his decision to step down had been the right one—even if it gave him an ache in his chest just thinking of handing Beth's future welfare over to any man other than himself.

Raphael drew himself up determinedly as he strode briskly into the kitchen, his gaze glacial as he glanced at the now-standing Rodney. 'Edward is ready to take us all to the airport if the two of you have quite finished your... conversation?'

Beth's eyes widened as she heard the condemnation in Raphael's tone. What the hell was wrong with him now? Now? There was nothing different about Raphael's briskly businesslike behaviour towards her this morning than any of the other mornings they had spent together.

She gave a cool nod. 'I'll just go upstairs and collect my bags.'

'They are already in the car,' Raphael informed her dismissively.

She gave a saccharin-sweet smile. 'Of course they are.'

Blue eyes narrowed on her piercingly. 'And what is that supposed to mean?'

Beth raised mocking brows. 'Exactly what it sounded like—admiration for Raphael Cordoba's efficiency.'

His lips thinned. 'Rodney has already explained that he will be taking over your security as from today?'

'Oh, yes.' She nodded coolly. 'And I can't tell you how

nice it is to know that I get on so well with the man I will
be spending so much time with in future.'

Raphael's jaw clenched. He had intended to tell Beth
over breakfast of the necessary changes that had been
made in her security detail—if not the reason for them!—
but she had looked so pale and unapproachable when she
joined him in the kitchen earlier, followed by his discomfort after their conversation regarding his estrangement
from his father, that he had thought it better to wait until
they were on the plane before breaking that particular piece
of news to her. He had not anticipated that Rodney would
see her first and impart that information to her.

Information which, if Beth's coolly contemptuous attitude towards Raphael now was any indication, she had
totally misinterpreted. A misunderstanding, and attitude,
that Rodney's presence made it impossible for Raphael
to try and explain or change. And asking to talk to Beth
alone—being alone with her for any reason—would not
be a wise move on Raphael's part when he still desired
her so deeply!

'As we are all ready, we may as well leave,' he bit out
tautly instead.

'The sooner the better,' Beth added hardly.

Raphael gave her a long and searching glance. She
really did look very pale. To the point of delicacy. Far too
much so, he believed, for it to be attributed solely to the
tension that now existed between the two of them.

Could he possibly have physically hurt Beth last night,
with the intensity of his lovemaking? Had he been too
rough with her? Too demanding?

'Would you wait outside for us in the car?' Raphael
instructed Rodney abruptly, his gaze still fixed unwaver-
ingly on the pallor of Beth's face.

She looked displeased at the idea of being alone with him. 'Oh, but—'

'Rodney,' Raphael prompted hardly, waiting until the other man had left the kitchen before turning back to a wide-eyed Beth. 'Are you feeling quite well?'

'Is that your not so polite way of telling me I look awful this morning?' she came back challengingly.

'Stop it, Beth!' Raphael reached out to lightly grasp the tops of her arms as he shook her slightly. 'You are very pale, that is all. I did not…hurt you, last night?'

Beth looked up at him sharply, her gaze searching on that aristocratically handsome face. Had Raphael somehow guessed? Did he *know* how she felt about him—?

'Physically?' His next harsh comment completely alleviated that particular worry.

She grimaced. 'I'm a little sore. But otherwise, no, you didn't hurt me.'

A frown creased his brow. 'I did not know—I was a little rough with you, considering your…innocence.'

'I really don't want to talk about this any more, Raphael!' Beth pulled out of his grasp, her gaze avoiding meeting that piercing blue one. 'I'm pale because I didn't sleep well, that's all. I'll sleep on the plane and be absolutely fine by the time we reach Buenos Aires.' She hoped.

That nagging pain in the pit of her stomach seemed to have spread to her side, too, now, and increased in intensity. So maybe their depth of lovemaking last night *had* somehow set off some sort of reaction inside her?

How embarrassing was that?

'Could we just go now, Raphael?' Her eyes flashed darkly as she looked up at him challengingly, heaving a relieved sigh as he gave a brief nod before indicating with his hand that she should precede him outside.

And with any luck, Beth could escape into that bedroom

at the back of the Navarro plane as soon as they had taken off, bury her head beneath the bedcovers, and just sleep for the whole tedious journey to Buenos Aires.

Well away from the disturbing Raphael Cordoba…

CHAPTER TWELVE

'BETH?' RAPHAEL SHOOK her gently by the shoulder as he sat down on the side of the bed in the cabin at the back of the Navarro jet, where Beth had disappeared to, and apparently been sleeping, almost from the moment the plane took off from England. 'Beth!' he repeated more firmly as he received no response.

She gave a groan as she turned onto her back and slowly opened her lids, her eyes appearing dark and slightly unfocused rather than the clear and challenging glitter Raphael was used to. 'Are we there?' She pushed back the long tangle of blond hair from her face.

'We will shortly begin our descent,' Raphael answered her distractedly: if anything Beth looked paler to him now than she had earlier. 'Are you still…in discomfort?' he amended tightly as he remembered her angry reaction to the last time they had this conversation.

'Oh, for heaven's sake, Raphael…!' She reacted just as impatiently this time, too, shooting him an irritated glance from beneath lowered brows as she pushed herself up against the pillows.

'I am merely concerned—'

'I'm fine!' Beth glared at him in the hopes of hiding her grimace of pain from him; far from going away, the pain in her side seemed to have got worse! 'What are you doing?' She flinched back as Raphael reached a hand out towards her.

'Checking to see if you have a temperature.' Raphael scowled at her reaction.

'I would be flushed, not pale, if I had a temperature,' she scoffed dismissively.

Raphael ignored her protests as he touched his hand against her forehead. 'You feel hot...'

'So would you if you'd had your head buried under the bedcovers for hours!' Beth swatted his hand away exasperatedly before pulling ineffectually at the bedcovers he sat on. 'For goodness' sake, move, Raphael, so that I can get out of bed and come through to the main cabin and strap myself in for landing.'

He remained exactly where he was as he continued to look at her frowningly. 'Perhaps I should call Cesar and ask him to have a doctor standing by for when we arrive—'

'And perhaps you should just do as I ask and go away,' Beth instructed through gritted teeth.

He stared at her in obvious frustration for several long seconds. A penetrating stare that Beth met head on, her chin raised stubbornly.

There was no way, absolutely no way, that she was going to admit to the amount of pain she was in. She certainly wasn't going to submit herself to some sort of internal examination—along with an embarrassing explanation as to why Raphael felt it was necessary—the moment she arrived at Cesar's apartment in Buenos Aires. Not only would that be too humiliating, it was likely to cause trouble between Cesar and Raphael.

She might be angry with Raphael, might inwardly wish that he felt the same way about her as she did him, but that didn't mean she wanted to cause a rift between Cesar and Raphael. As there was sure to be if Cesar learnt just how close she and her bodyguard—*former* bodyguard—had become these past few days.

Raphael gave a shake of his head. 'I do not believe this amount of…discomfort is normal, in these circumstances—'

'I don't want to hear what is or isn't normal "in these circumstances".' Beth continued to glare at him. 'Or how you happen to know what's normal,' she muttered irritably. 'I'm a little sore from last night, and slightly hot from sleeping under the bedcovers, but that's it.'

'If you are sure?'

'I'm so sure that if you don't soon leave then I swear I'm going to start screaming,' she threatened.

Raphael stood up abruptly. 'Your bad-temperedness in the mornings obviously extends to whatever time of day you wake up.'

Beth gave a reluctant smile. 'Nice to know you were listening to me.'

'Oh, I always listen to you, Beth,' he murmured huskily. 'Even when what you are saying is not pleasant.'

She gave him a sharp look. Did Raphael know how she felt about him, after all? And was his answer, to realising she was in love with him, to immediately put Rodney in his place as her bodyguard? God, was the humiliation never going to end?

'Fine,' she bit out abruptly. 'Well, what I'm saying now is that I'm perfectly okay, and that I just need a couple of minutes' privacy to freshen myself up, and then I'll join you and Rodney in the main cabin.'

'Very well.' He gave a terse inclination of his head. 'But if you are not improved by the time we get to Cesar's— Do not scream!' he bit out harshly as Beth opened her mouth to do exactly that.

She gave an unrepentant shrug. 'Can't say I haven't warned you.'

No, Raphael could not claim that at all; Beth was a woman who always did what she said she was going to do. Including screaming, if he didn't leave immediately and give her the privacy she asked for.

Which in no way changed the fact that, whether Beth liked it or not, Raphael had every intention of talking to Cesar if she seemed no better by the time they reached her brother's apartment.

A conversation that would no doubt for ever damn him in Cesar's eyes, as well as Beth's…

'Beth…! Oh, my God, Beth!' Esther pulled her into a fierce and emotional hug the moment Beth stepped into the hallway of Cesar's apartment, the other woman's body shaking slightly as she burst into unashamed tears.

Beth hesitated for only a fraction of a second before she wrapped her own arms about Esther, tears blurring her vision as she clung to the woman who was her mother, wanting, somehow needing, that comfort at this moment. 'I'm sorry. So sorry that I wouldn't believe you before—'

'And I'm sorry you had to go through the trauma of yesterday alone.' Esther groaned as her arms tightened. 'I should have been there for you…!'

'I wasn't alone, Raphael was there,' Beth soothed, knowing, no matter how strained their relationship might be now, that without the strength of Raphael's quiet support visiting Elizabeth Lawrence's graveside yesterday would have been every bit as traumatic as Esther thought it was. 'And it seems to me,' she continued huskily, 'that you've been there for me, waiting for me to return, for the past twenty-one years.' She glanced over Esther's shoulder and saw Carlos standing in the doorway of the sitting room, tears of happiness glistening in his dark eyes so like her own. 'Both of you have,' she added emotionally as she removed one of her arms from about Esther's waist to hold her hand out to Carlos.

Carlos didn't hesitate as he stepped forward to tightly grasp her hand in his. 'Brela…!'

Beth gave him a tearful smile. 'Papa.' She used the same term of address she had heard Cesar use with their parents, surprised—overjoyed—at how right it sounded, and without feeling in the least a betrayal of the love the Lawrences and the Blakes had shown her for so many years. She had called the Lawrences 'Mummy and Daddy' and the Blakes 'Mum and Dad'. She smiled tremulously at Esther. 'Mama.'

Esther gave another choked sob as Carlos gathered both women in his arms and hugged them tightly to his chest. As if he never wanted, or intended, to let them go ever again.

How long the three of them remained that way Beth had no idea, clinging tightly to Esther and Carlos as she felt something inside her give way, collapse completely— a door opening into her heart?—to allow these two wonderful people inside.

These were her parents. The mother who had carried her in her womb for nine months, the two wonderful people who had loved and nurtured her for the first two years of her life, who had continued to love, to mourn, the daughter they had lost so many years ago. As Cesar was her brother—

Beth looked up and saw him standing in the same doorway where their father had been only seconds ago, a tall and imperiously arrogant man, and yet there was that same bright sheen of tears glinting in his dark eyes. 'You, too,

'Zar,' she encouraged huskily as she held her hand out to him.

'Brela…!' he choked even as he stepped forward to wrap his arms about all of them, the two Navarro men cradling their women within the protective circle of their arms. 'Oh, God, Brela!'

Raphael stood off to one side watching this exchange, more happy than he could ever have expressed at seeing the Navarro family reunited at long last.

'Thank you so much for all that you've done, Raphael.'

Raphael glanced down at Grace Blake as she moved to stand beside him, tears falling hotly down her cheeks as she watched her adopted sister being embraced by the man who was her brother—and also the man who would soon become Grace's own husband—and Beth's real mother and father, the couple who would shortly become Grace's own mother- and father-in-law. It was, Raphael decided, a fitting solution to a situation that could have proved so delicately awkward.

He gave a shake of his head. 'I did very little.'

'I don't believe that for a moment.' Grace gave a firm shake of her head.

He gave Grace an indulgent smile. 'Why is it that you Blake women never have a handkerchief when you need one?' he teased softly as he pulled a neatly folded white silk handkerchief from his pocket and handed it to Grace.

She mopped up the worst of her deluge of tears, a frown now between her blue-green eyes. 'Beth has been crying?'

'Naturally so.' Raphael nodded.

Grace glanced across at her adopted sister. 'I'm so proud of her for the way she's now dealing with all this.'

Raphael felt equally proud—unaccountably so, when he was a complete outsider to this emotional reunion—

of the way in which Beth had at last embraced who she really was.

At the same time as he knew an inward sadness, at the distance that now stood between the two of them…

'Yes,' he agreed huskily as he continued to look at Beth as she talked softly, and laughed and cried, with the three people who were her family.

'Are you okay, Raphael?'

He arched one dark questioning brow as he turned to look at Grace, a shutter coming down over his emotions as he saw the concern in her expression. 'Why would I not be okay?' he broached guardedly.

'I don't know…' She gave a slow shake of her head as she continued to look up at him searchingly. 'You look… tired. Or maybe a little sad?'

Raphael frowned at the extent of this woman's intuition. He was very tired, and not just from the lack of sleep the past two days; his army training had ensured that he could endure several days without sleep and still remain alert and ready for anything that was thrown at him.

His present weariness was for quite another reason.

The mature way in which Beth had now embraced her real family—literally—brought into sharp contrast Raphael's own strained relationship with his father. A strain that Raphael had allowed to continue as much as his father had. And it was past time for that breach to be healed.

It had taken Beth, with her unshakeable candour, for him to see that.

As for the sadness Grace believed she detected in him…

Raphael glanced back at Beth. She still seemed unnaturally pale to him, but at the same time she had never looked more beautiful to him, either. Not just her obvious outer beauty, but that inner strength she carried with her so innately, the ability she had to meet any situation head on and deal with it, at the same time as she was able to inspire laughter and warmth in those around her.

'Raphael?'

He turned to give Grace a reassuring smile. 'I believe I am simply in need of a holiday.'

'Cesar said you'd requested a couple of weeks' leave. I trust you'll be back in time for the wedding next month?' she added teasingly.

'As Cesar has asked me to stand beside him in the church, I had better be,' he confirmed dryly.

Grace nodded. 'Are you going anywhere nice?'

Raphael did not believe his planned visit to his father's *estacia*—ranch—would be in the least nice. Necessary, but far from nice! 'Just visiting family,' he dismissed easily. 'Rodney will be here to take care of Beth's security.'

'It's nice to see Rodney again.' Grace gave a wry chuckle. 'I still remember the incredulous look on Cesar's face the day I suggested he might like to have Rodney shoot me and have me buried in the grounds of the estate in Hampshire!'

'I believe Cesar mentioned that incident to me.' Raphael gave a throaty chuckle.

'Laughing while he did it, no doubt!' She grimaced.

'I believe he was slightly amused by the notion, yes,' Raphael acknowledged dryly.

Grace nodded, her eyes glowing as she glanced across at Cesar. 'It seems incredible that the two of us are now in love and going to be married next month.'

'I have never seen Cesar happier than he has been since you agreed to become his wife,' Raphael assured her huskily.

Grace gave him a glowing smile. 'Thank you.'

Raphael only stated the truth; his own close friendship with Cesar had existed since their schooldays together, making it easy for him to see that Grace's love had completed Cesar, filling the voids of loneliness that had existed inside him for so long, at the same time as she had rubbed away all the hard edges that had kept Cesar removed and so distant from the world around him.

In the same way that Beth had rubbed those same edges of detachment from Raphael?

Beth, glancing across at Raphael and Grace as they stood quietly talking together further down the hallway, couldn't help but frown as she saw how easily the two of them were laughing together. The sort of companionable ease that Beth wished she and Raphael had together, but knew they never would.

She not only wanted him physically but had fallen in love with him, and although the night at the inn had proved that Raphael returned that physical attraction, his every action since had shown her that he certainly wasn't in love with her.

Just looking at him now, and knowing how much she loved him, made Beth's heart ache. Almost enough to take her mind off the nagging, insistent ache in her side!

A nagging and insistent ache that made her feel physically sick, and which she knew owed nothing, absolutely nothing, to the pain of the unrequited love she felt for Raphael.

She kept her arm about Esther's waist as she pulled back slightly.

'Would anyone mind if I went to my room to lie down for a while? This past couple of days have been a bit... emotional, and I'm feeling a little tired,' she added ruefully.

'I'll come with you,' Grace offered huskily.

'I would like that.' Beth turned to smile at her sister as she joined them, a quick glance behind Grace showing her that Raphael was nowhere in sight. 'Has Raphael gone?' she prompted with as much lightness as she could muster—and instantly knowing she hadn't fooled Grace for a moment as her sister's gaze narrowed on her speculatively. Beth never had been able to hide anything from Grace for very long!

Including the way she now felt about Raphael, apparently.

'He said there were a couple of things he had to do,' Grace answered her slowly.

Of course he did. Raphael might have transferred her personal security to Rodney, but he was still Head of Security worldwide for Cesar, with all of the responsibilities that went along with that job description.

'You go and rest now and we'll see you later, honey.' Esther touched Beth's cheek gently as she smiled at her.

'*Querida.*' Carlos kissed her warmly on her other cheek.

'Brela.' Cesar lifted her hand and kissed the back of it.

Making the emotion catch in the back of Beth's throat all over again. Not only would she always have Grace as her sister, but she now had this wonderful family as her own, too. Her cup wasn't just half full, it was overflowing.

Apart, of course, from the fact that she was in love with a man who was never going to fall in love with her...

'Okay, what's going on?' Grace prompted shrewdly once the two sisters were alone together in the same bedroom they had shared the last time Beth had visited Buenos Aires and stayed at Cesar's apartment.

Just days ago, and yet those days had been life changing for Beth. In more ways than one! 'Going on?' she prompted with that same attempt at lightness as earlier as she lay down on one of the single beds in the room—and with just

as much success if the look of scepticism on Grace's face
was any indication!

'Between you and Raphael.' Grace nodded as she
dropped down onto the other bed. 'He's walking around
with a face like thunder and trying not to look at you too
often, and you have a permanent false smile fixed on your
face—while also trying to give the appearance of not looking at him, either!'

Beth grimaced. 'You're imagining things.'

'Don't try that with me, Beth,' her sister warned ruefully. 'I know you far too well for you to get away with it.
And, for some reason, you and Raphael are both trying to
give the appearance that neither one of you believes the
other exists.'

As usual, her sister had gone straight to the heart of the
problem! 'I think you have that slightly wrong, Grace. I'm
only too well aware that Raphael exists—he's the one trying to ignore me.'

'Why?'

Beth gave a grimace as the twinge of pain in her side
gave a particularly vicious twist. 'Because he doesn't like
or approve of me any more now than he did four days ago?'

Grace gave her a reproving look. 'We both know that
isn't it.'

'Do we?'

Her sister sighed. 'Okay, you obviously don't want to
talk about this right now. But when you do,' she continued before Beth could relax her guard too much, 'know
that I'm here for you.'

'Always,' Beth acknowledged huskily.

Grace nodded. 'And that I don't judge.'

She felt the tears well up in her eyes. For what had
to be the hundredth time today. 'I'm just so emotionally

exhausted at the moment, Grace, that I can barely see straight, let alone talk coherently,' she admitted gruffly.

'I can see that.' Her sister stood up to pat one of her hands sympathetically. 'You're looking a little pale?'

'Don't you start!' She grimaced. 'Raphael has done nothing else today but tell me how awful I look!'

'I'm sure he didn't mean it in the way you've obviously taken it.' Grace still studied her worriedly.

'I admire your optimism!'

'We'll talk again later, hmm?' Grace soothed softly. 'And maybe this couple of weeks apart from Raphael will...help resolve whatever appears to have gone wrong between the two of you.'

'He's only turned my personal security over to Rodney, Grace,' she dismissed lightly. 'I'm sure I'll still see his annoying presence about the apartment.'

Her sister gave a slow shake of her head. 'He didn't tell you?'

Beth raised her brows. 'Tell me what?'

'That he's taken two weeks' leave, effective immediately. In fact,' Grace added with a frown as Beth gasped softly, 'I wouldn't be surprised if he hasn't already gone.'

Gone?

Raphael had gone?

From Cesar's apartment, possibly even Buenos Aires?

Without so much as telling her, let alone saying goodbye...

It was the screaming that woke Beth. A loud and piercing scream. And it was obviously a pained scream rather than one of fear.

And she wanted it to stop.

Now.

Wanted to just stay in her dream state, safe from the memories, the hurt, of Raphael's defection.

Except the screaming was getting louder.

And louder.

'Beth, wake up!' Grace's panicked voice pierced the last layers of Beth's sleep as she felt her shoulder being shaken. 'Beth, wake up now and tell me what's wrong!'

Which was when Beth realised that *she* was the one screaming.

A pained scream rather than one of fear.

A ripping, roaring pain that began in her side and radiated out to her stomach.

She opened her eyes wide to stare up at a white-faced Grace. 'It hurts, Grace! Oh, God, it hurts!' she managed to gasp before the pain became too much, too unbearable, and the blackness carried her away...

CHAPTER THIRTEEN

'IT'S BEEN TWO days now, Doctor.'

Beth frowned as she heard Grace talking to…a doctor? Why was Grace talking to a doctor? And why did she sound so worried?

'You said she would wake up soon.' Grace's voice became even more strained.

Beth knew instinctively that the 'she' her sister was talking about was her, and she desperately wanted to open her eyes, to reassure Grace that she was fine, that she *was* awake. But her lids felt so heavy. Too heavy for Beth to raise them, no matter how hard she tried, just as her throat felt too dry for her to be able to talk. And yet she knew that she had to open her eyes, had to talk, that she had to reassure Grace. Had to—

'Of course, Miss Blake, but, as I explained to you this morning, the body takes its own time to recover…' A voice, one Beth didn't recognise, became a low and distant murmur, as did Grace's hushed reply, and there was the soft click of a door closing.

Indicating that they were no longer in the room?

Beth's hands clenched into fists at her sides as she desperately searched her memory in an effort to understand what was going on. She remembered flying back to Argentina. Remembered going to her bedroom in Cesar's apartment. Remembered Grace telling her that Raphael had gone away. Vividly remembered the screams that had awoken her hours later. The realisation that *she* was the one screaming.

The pain!

Oh, God, Beth remembered the pain now. Pain unlike anything she had ever known before. Before she had been swept away in a whirl of dark and thankful oblivion.

Grace had mentioned something about 'two days'. Did that mean that the screaming, the pain, the oblivion, had all happened two days ago? And if so—

'It's time to open your eyes now, Beth.'

Beth didn't so much open her eyes as widen them in astonishment, before turning in the direction of that huskily low voice. A voice she recognised all too easily. Just as she easily recognised the man standing in the shadowed darkness as he leant so casually against the wall several feet away from where she lay in bed. Raphael!

'You aren't supposed to be here.' She was sure it was her own voice speaking, because she could feel her lips moving, but the sound that came out of those lips sounded more like a rasping croak than her normal light tones.

'It is good to see you again, too!' Raphael drawled hardly as he pushed away from the wall to step into the soft glow of light given off by that lamp on the wall above Beth's head.

A Raphael with at least a one-day darkness of stubble on the squareness of his jaw, his cheeks slightly hollow— even his military-style short dark hair looked as if it was slightly mussed and in need of a trim. His eyes were the same piercing blue, and his shoulders looked as broad and his chest as muscled beneath the fitted black T-shirt he wore, with faded denims fitting low down on his hips.

Beth tried to moisten her lips before speaking again, but her mouth was so dry that it was a wasted effort.

'Would you like some water?' Raphael looked at her intently with those piercing blue eyes.

'Yes, please,' she accepted gratefully, attempting to sit up and failing miserably. She simply didn't have the strength to lift herself up, and even the slight movement she had managed to make had been enough to tell her that her side still ached. Not as it had before, but enough so that Beth knew something was dreadfully wrong. 'What's happening to me?' she demanded emotionally.

His expression softened. 'Nothing now. Here.' He put one of his arms beneath her shoulders to help her to sit up enough so that she could drink through a straw some of the water that he had poured into the bottom of a glass. 'Better?' he prompted gently once she had emptied the glass.

'Much.' Beth sank wearily back onto the pillows before looking about the room in which she lay. A pleasant but totally sterile-looking room that she didn't recognise. 'This is a hospital.' She looked up at Raphael.

'It is, yes.' He nodded as he turned back from placing the empty glass on the side table, his expression appearing harsh in the shadowed lamplight. 'Your discomfort three days ago was not because of—' He gave a shake of his head. 'You were in pain for several days because your appendix was infected. Two nights ago it decided to burst.'

She swallowed before speaking again. 'That can be dangerous, can't it?'

'Very,' he confirmed grimly.

Beth gave him a teasing frown. 'Aren't you supposed to murmur reassurances rather than scare me?'

Raphael looked no less grim. 'Not when you scared everyone else! You almost died, Beth,' he added gratingly.

'Well, I obviously didn't,' she dismissed, distracted.

The water had revived her slightly, enough for her to feel thankful that someone—Grace?—had ensured she was at least wearing a pair of her own pyjamas rather than one of those unflattering hospital gowns. Although her hair was probably a mess, and— What did it matter what she looked like? This man—Raphael—had walked away from her two—no, three—nights ago, without so much as a goodbye.

Her jaw tensed as she looked up at him challengingly. 'What are you doing here, Raphael? Have you come back to make sure that it really wasn't the discomfort of the other night that had made me ill?'

Raphael drew in a hissing breath. 'Perhaps we should have asked them to remove your viperous tongue at the same time as they removed your appendix!'

'Perhaps you should.' She continued to look up at him challengingly.

Raphael bit back his second angry retort as he remembered that Beth had almost died on the operating table two nights ago. That it had taken every shred of expertise the surgeon possessed to ensure that she did not. 'My presence here is obviously upsetting you—'

'Not in the least,' she dismissed dryly. 'I'm merely wondering why you're here at all?'

A good question. And one that required an answer. But not here. And not now. Not when the Navarro family and Grace were all outside in the corridor talking to the doctor as they anxiously waited for Beth to regain consciousness.

Raphael gave a shake of his head. 'I have to tell your family that you are awake.'

'Which doesn't answer my question in the slightest,' Beth persisted. 'You went away, Raphael. Took two weeks leave. Without so much as a—' She broke off as her voice quivered with emotion. 'You handed my security over to Rodney, and then you went away,' she repeated dully.

He frowned. 'But I was coming back.'

'When your two weeks' leave were over.' She nodded. 'Which is why I asked what you're doing here now.'

That was some reassurance at least; Raphael had thought Beth's initial comment to mean that she didn't want him here, and not that he shouldn't be here because he was on leave. He reached out and lightly clasped one of her hands in his. 'I came back as soon as Cesar told me that you were in hospital.'

A frown appeared between her eyes. 'Came back from where? And how could he have told you anything when you were away?'

'He told me after I had telephoned the apartment yesterday and asked to speak with you.'

She blinked. 'Speak to me about what?'

Raphael drew in a deep breath. 'I wanted— I owed it to you to tell you that I had taken your advice and gone to see my father.'

Her eyes widened. 'And is everything…all right between the two of you now?'

'Yes. Beth, I—' Raphael stopped what he had been about to say as he heard Esther's voice just outside the door. 'Your family will want to be with you now.' He released her hand. 'The two of us will talk once you are home and feeling better.'

Now that Beth was fully awake, and remembered— remembered being with Raphael at the inn, realising how much she loved him, and how he had walked away from her without so much as a goodbye, she wasn't sure she would ever feel completely 'better' again. Oh, no doubt, now that she had regained consciousness, she would very quickly recover from the operation to remove her infected appendix. It was the pain in her heart, her love and longing for Raphael, that would never heal...

She raised her chin. 'I'm really pleased, about you and your father, Raphael, but I don't think we have anything else left to talk about.'

He blinked those long-lashed lids over those piercing blue eyes. 'You wish me to leave?'

Beth nodded abruptly. 'I believe that would be for the best.'

A nerve pulsed in his tightly clenched jaw. 'If you are sure that is what you want?'

'It is,' she bit out softly.

'Very well.' He stepped back from the bedside. 'I will send your family in now.'

Beth refused to look at him again as she heard the softness of his tread as he crossed the room to the door, the door softly opening, followed by a brief conversation outside before her family rushed to her bedside and she laughingly gave them her reassurances that she really was okay.

There would be all the time in the world for tears later...

'Beth, he came back to Buenos Aires the moment Cesar told him you were in the hospital,' Grace admonished softly.

Beth didn't turn from where she sat convalescing beside one of the windows in the sitting room of Cesar's apartment. But she knew who the 'he' was that Grace was referring to. The same 'he' who had been asking to visit her since she came home from the hospital two days ago. The same 'he' that Beth had turned away each and every time Grace came in to tell her that Raphael was outside asking to see her.

'Beth—'

'I can't, Grace!' She turned to her sister fiercely. 'Don't you understand? I can't see him…!' she choked.

Grace crossed the room until she was able to go down on her haunches beside Beth. 'You love him.'

Beth breathed raggedly. 'Yes.'

'Then—'

'He doesn't feel the same way about me, Grace.' She sighed. 'He— I don't know why he came back from his father's ranch. Or why he keeps asking to see me now. A guilty conscience maybe? But I can't—!' She gave a fierce shake of her head, her hands tightly clasped together in her lap.

'Why should Raphael have a guilty conscience where you're concerned?' Grace looked at her searchingly.

Beth drew in a deep and shaky breath. 'I'm sure you can guess why. He thought— He originally thought that the pain I was in had been caused by—' Her cheeks flushed a fiery red as she shook her head. 'He thought he had hurt me in some way. I told him he hadn't, but he kept fussing, and—'

'That still doesn't explain why he keeps asking to see you now,' Grace maintained firmly.

Beth looked at her searchingly. 'Don't you have something to say about—about my…closeness, to Raphael?'

'Why should I?' her sister returned lightly. 'You're a big girl now, and quite capable of making up your own mind about who you go to bed with.'

'I didn't— We didn't—' Beth gave a pained frown. 'We didn't get that far,' she admitted uncomfortably.

'Even more reason for me to question why Raphael rushed back here the moment Cesar told him you had been taken to hospital, and refused to leave your bedside once he arrived back.'

'He must have gone to the bathroom occasionally—'

'Beth!'

She grimaced. 'I don't know why Raphael did that. Maybe he felt it was his duty, as Cesar's Head of Security, to rush back and protect Cesar's little sister while she was in hospital?'

Grace gave her an admonishing glance. 'Aren't you even a little bit curious as to why he's asked to see you a dozen times since you got home?'

Was Beth curious as to why Raphael had asked to see her these past two days? Of course she was curious! But every time she gave in to that curiosity she remembered that Raphael had discharged his responsibility for her security onto Rodney after they had returned from the inn in Surrey. That he had left to visit his father without so much as a goodbye as soon as they had returned to Argentina. There was only so much pain an already broken heart could take, and her heart had been shattered the moment she knew she was so unimportant to Raphael he had left without saying that goodbye.

'Yes, Beth, are you not curious as to why I continue to humiliate myself by *asking* if you will see me, knowing you will once again refuse me, when my every instinct *demands* that you allow me to speak with you?'

Beth's head had snapped round towards the sound of that angry voice the moment Raphael first spoke, and she took a few seconds now to drink in the sight of him. His hair was once again neat and tidy, his jaw shaven, and yet there was still that strain about his eyes and mouth, the hollowness to his cheeks. And he was wearing one of those perfectly tailored three-piece suits and a pristine white shirt and grey silk tie, but it was still possible to see that he had lost weight in the week since she had seen him last.

Because he had asked to see her and she had refused him?

She somehow didn't think so!

'I'll leave the two of you to talk.' Grace straightened.

Beth didn't take her gaze off the grim-faced Raphael. 'We have nothing to talk about—'

'Stop being so damned stubborn for once in your life and just listen to the man. You might actually learn something!' Grace snapped reprovingly, turning on her heel to step around Raphael before leaving the room and closing the door softly but firmly behind her.

Leaving behind a speechless Beth. The two sisters had both been adopted by the Blakes, but they had bonded from the moment they first met, and Grace never lost her temper with her. Never, no matter how much Beth's impulsiveness had annoyed or upset her.

'Why does that never work for me?' Raphael chuckled wryly as he stepped further into the room.

Her eyes flashed darkly. 'Probably because—'

'No, do not spoil it, Beth,' he cajoled softly. 'At least let me have my say before you throw me out again.'

'I thought we had agreed we have nothing to say to each other.'

'No, Beth, you said we had not, I did not agree. It was only—' He began to pace the room restlessly. 'The hospital, with your family all waiting outside, was not the time for this conversation. And you have refused to see me since you came home.' He scowled darkly.

'Because—'

'I have not finished, Beth.'

She drew in a deep breath. 'Okay.' She nodded. 'Say what you have to say, and then will you leave me alone?'

'I am hoping not, no…' Raphael looked down at her searchingly, Beth looked much better than she had a week ago when he last saw her at the hospital, but there was still a fine delicacy to the paleness of her face, and she looked as if she had lost weight, her denims and T-shirt slightly too large on her slender frame. It was natural to lose some weight after an operation, of course, but Raphael found he did not like to see her looking so delicate. Not his fiery Beth.

Except she was not his Beth…

'You said some things to me in the hospital that I feel need an explanation. Not from you,' he reassured her, 'but from me. You seem to be under the impression that I passed your security to Rodney because I no longer wished to be anywhere near you.'

A slight blush entered her cheeks. 'Well, didn't you?'

'No.'

She looked up at him uncertainly. 'No?'

'No,' Raphael repeated grimly. 'I handed your security to Rodney because I no longer trusted myself to be…impartial, where your security is concerned.'

Beth gave a slow shake of her head. 'I don't understand.'

'Obviously not,' he acknowledged grimly. 'And I did not say goodbye to you before I left because if I had I would not have been able to leave! And I needed to do so. I had to talk to my father, to attempt to heal the rift between the two of us, before I could move forward with my life.'

'And did you?'

'Yes.' He nodded.

She gave a tremulous smile. 'I'm glad.'

So was Raphael. He had barely spent more than a few hours with his father before learning Beth had been rushed to hospital, but it had nevertheless been long enough for the two proud Cordoba men to reconcile. A reconciliation he had wanted to share with Beth, only to telephone the apartment to instead learn that she was seriously ill. The drive back from his father's *estancia* had been a nightmare as he feared for Beth's very life.

A chilling fear, which had told him all that he needed to know in regard to his feelings for Beth.

He reached out and took one of her hands in his. 'Beth, so much has happened in your life in such a short time. You have discovered that you are not who you thought you were, but someone else entirely. And that you have a family, a family you were not aware of, who love you very much.'

She eyed him uncertainly. 'Yes…'

Raphael straightened to once again pace restlessly. 'Now is not really the time for me to— I should not—this is much more difficult than I would ever have believed possible!'

'Maybe if you were to tell me what it is I could help you out a little?' Beth prompted curiously.

He gave a slightly impatient shake of his head. 'Can it be that you are the only one who has not realised what I want to say?'

She looked at him blankly. 'About what? I'm really pleased that you and your father have made your peace—'

'Beth, this has absolutely nothing to do with my relationship with my father!' he interrupted exasperatedly. 'Well, maybe a little,' he conceded impatiently. 'I had to… resolve that part of my life, make things right with my father, before I could—'

'Move forward with your life.' She nodded. 'Yes, you said that.'

'Move forward with my life with you!' Raphael's voice rose and he ran his hand through his hair in his frustration. '*Madre mia,* woman, the whole of your family knows that the reason I have tried to see you this past week is because I need to tell you that I am in love with you. So very very much in love with you. That I realised this the night we spent together at the inn. That I wish, above all things, that you would love me, too. That I wish to ask you to become my wife. Once you are completely well again, of course.' He frowned. 'And once you feel that you could leave your new family. And—'

'And after Grace and Cesar's wedding. And after their first child has been christened.' Her eyes glowed. 'And man has settled on Mars—'

'I do not understand…' Raphael looked pained as he stood beside her chair looking down at her.

Beth gave a choked laugh as the happiness welled up inside her and threatened to totally overwhelm her. Raphael loved her. He wanted to marry her. All this time she had been suffering in misery, believing he would never feel the same way about her, and Raphael had been in love with her the whole time, too. To the point that he hadn't felt able to protect her in the way he felt she needed to be protected. To a degree that he had decided to settle the long feud with his father, to resolve the rift between the two of them, before he asked Beth to marry him.

Raphael loved her and wanted to marry her!

She moved to stand up, needing to be in Raphael's arms, only to sit back down again with a wince. 'Ouch.' She made a pained face. 'Raphael, will you get down here and kiss me before I rip my stitches open trying to get to you?'

'But—'

'Now, please!' she cried frustratedly.

'You are a very demanding woman,' he reproved as he moved to sit on the arm of her chair.

'No, you stubborn arrogant man, I'm a woman in love,' she corrected happily as she raised her face to his. 'Very, very much in love. With you. And my ridiculous comments just now were because I have no intention of waiting for any of those things to happen before becoming your wife—my answer is yes now, Raphael,' she assured him softly as he lowered his head towards hers.

He paused with his lips only centimetres away from hers as he looked down at her searchingly. 'I have yet to ask the question…' he murmured softly.

'But you will. And when you do my answer will be yes,' she assured him as she raised her hand and cupped his nape. 'I love you, Raphael. So very much.'

'And I love you, too, my Beth,' he answered gruffly before his lips at last claimed hers.

And a long, long time later Raphael did ask her to marry him, and she said yes…

All of the Navarro and Cordoba families attended the wedding three months later.

Beth walked down the aisle on Carlos's arm, and behind her walked her sister, Grace, as matron of honour, and beside her was Raphael's sister Rosa, as bridesmaid. Esther sat on one side of the aisle, and beamed proudly at the same time as the tears of happiness streamed unashamedly down her cheeks. And on the other side of the aisle sat Raphael Cordoba senior, Raphael's father, his dark eyes gleaming with pride for his son, and affection for the woman he already loved like another daughter.

When Beth emerged from the church an hour later on Raphael's arm she was no longer Beth Lawrence, or Beth Blake, or even Gabriela Navarro, but Beth Cordoba, wife of Raphael Cordoba, the man she loved, and would continue to love with all of her heart for the rest of her life, and the man who vowed he would love and cherish her with that same total commitment for the rest of his life.

She was, and always would be, Beth, Raphael Cordoba's wife.

* * * * *

#3149 DIAMOND IN THE DESERT
Susan Stephens

With the future of the Skavanga diamond mine in jeopardy, heiress Britt Skavanga needs an injection of cash—fast. She finds it in the mysterious Arabian investor known only as *Emir*...but his exacting fee is not financial!

#3150 A GREEK ESCAPE
Elizabeth Power

Jilted by her cheating boyfriend, her self-esteem in tatters, Kayla Young escapes to an isolated Greek island. But the last thing she wants is to have to share her precious paradise with the mysterious, arrogant Leonidas Vassalio.

#3151 A THRONE FOR THE TAKING
Royal & Ruthless
Kate Walker

Betrayed by those she loves, Honoria Escalona must face the only man capable of bringing stability to the kingdom of Mecjoria. But Alexei Sarova's past has changed him into someone she hardly knows, and his help comes with a price....

#3152 PRINCESS IN THE IRON MASK
Victoria Parker

Dispatched by the king to retrieve his headstrong daughter, Lucas Garcia thought this was just another day at the office. That's before he meets Princess Claudine, who's adamant that returning to her father's kingdom is never going to happen!

You can find more information on upcoming Harlequin® titles, free excerpts and more at www.Harlequin.com.

REQUEST YOUR FREE BOOKS!

2 FREE NOVELS PLUS
2 FREE GIFTS!

YES! Please send me 2 FREE Harlequin Presents® novels and my 2 FREE gifts (gifts are worth about $10). After receiving them, if I don't wish to receive any more books, I can return the shipping statement marked "cancel." If I don't cancel, I will receive 6 brand-new novels every month and be billed just $4.30 per book in the U.S. or $4.99 per book in Canada. That's a saving of at least 14% off the cover price! It's quite a bargain! Shipping and handling is just 50¢ per book in the U.S. and 75¢ per book in Canada.* I understand that accepting the 2 free books and gifts places me under no obligation to buy anything. I can always return a shipment and cancel at any time. Even if I never buy another book, the two free books and gifts are mine to keep forever.

106/306 HDN FVRK

Name	(PLEASE PRINT)	
Address		Apt. #
City	State/Prov.	Zip/Postal Code

Signature (if under 18, a parent or guardian must sign)

Mail to the **Harlequin® Reader Service:**
IN U.S.A.: P.O. Box 1867, Buffalo, NY 14240-1867
IN CANADA: P.O. Box 609, Fort Erie, Ontario L2A 5X3

Are you a current subscriber to Harlequin Presents books
and want to receive the larger-print edition?
Call 1-800-873-8635 or visit www.ReaderService.com.

* Terms and prices subject to change without notice. Prices do not include applicable taxes. Sales tax applicable in N.Y. Canadian residents will be charged applicable taxes. Offer not valid in Quebec. This offer is limited to one order per household. Not valid for current subscribers to Harlequin Presents books. All orders subject to credit approval. Credit or debit balances in a customer's account(s) may be offset by any other outstanding balance owed by or to the customer. Please allow 4 to 6 weeks for delivery. Offer available while quantities last.

Your Privacy—The Harlequin® Reader Service is committed to protecting your privacy. Our Privacy Policy is available online at www.ReaderService.com or upon request from the Harlequin Reader Service.

We make a portion of our mailing list available to reputable third parties that offer products we believe may interest you. If you prefer that we not exchange your name with third parties, or if you wish to clarify or modify your communication preferences, please visit us at www.ReaderService.com/consumerchoice or write to us at Harlequin Reader Service Preference Service, P.O. Box 9062, Buffalo, NY 14269. Include your complete name and address.

HP13

SPECIAL EXCERPT FROM

HARLEQUIN®

Presents

*Dispatched by the king to retrieve his headstrong
daughter, Lucas Garcia thought this was just another day
at the office…until he meets Princess Claudine Verbault.*

*Enjoy a sneak preview of PRINCESS IN THE IRON MASK
by debut author Victoria Parker.*

* * *

"You barge into my life and proceed to conduct some sort
of military operation. And now you're going on like an
interfering, dictatorial knave!"

Suddenly Lucas stopped and turned on his heels to face
her. "Do you have an aversion to authority, Claudia? Is that
what this is? You don't like being told what to do?"

The gray silken weave of his tailored suit began to turn
black as the rain seeped through his clothing. His overlong
hair was already dripping and plastered to his smooth forehead and the high slash of his cheekbones. And the sight of
him, wet and disheveled, flooded her with heat. Like this he
was far more powerful and dangerous to her equilibrium.
He looked gloriously untamed.

"No, actually, I don't. Do you think it's right to force
someone against their every wish? To blackmail in order
to do your job?" Something dark flashed in his eyes, but
she was too far gone to care. "And because I dare to put up
some sort of fight, you deem me selfish and irresponsible.
Do you have any feelings?"

"I am not paid to feel," he ground out, taking a step closer toward her.

"It's a good job, 'cos you'd be broke," she replied, taking a step back.

Lucas pinched the bridge of his nose with his thumb and forefinger. "You're the most provoking woman I have ever met."

A mere two feet away, Claudia could feel the heat radiating from his broad torso. Oh God, she had to get away from him before she did something seriously stupid. Like smooth her hands up his soaked shirt. "You know what, Lucas? I'm staying here."

Before he could say another word, she bolted sideways. Only to be blocked by a one-arm barricade.

"Over my dead body," he growled, corralling her back toward the car.

* * *

Find out who will win the battle of wills in
PRINCESS IN THE IRON MASK by Victoria Parker,
available May 21, 2013.

HPEXP0513-I